The Villain Kids' Guide

FOR NEW VKs

Art by Devin Taylor

Design by Lindsay Broderick

Editorial by Bonnie Steele

Copyright © 2019 Disney Enterprises, Inc.

Printed in the United States of America

First Hardcover Edition, July 2019

1 3 5 7 9 10 8 6 4 2

Library of Congress Control Number: 2019933991

ISBN 978-1-368-04704-3

FAC-038091-19144

For more Disney Press fun, visit www.disneybooks.com

Visit DisneyChannel.com

SUSTAINABLE FORESTRY INITIATIVE

Certified Sourcing

www.sfiprogram.org

SFI-00993

Logo Applies to Text Stock Only

Disney DESCENDANTS 3

The Villain Kids' Guide FOR NEW VKs

ADAPTED BY TINA McLEEF

BASED ON THE FILM BY

JOSANN McGIBBON & SARA PARRIOTT

DISNEY PRESS

LOS ANGELES • NEW YORK

Congratulations! This is your official acceptance letter and welcome packet for Auradon Prep. Your application was carefully reviewed and you were chosen based on your accomplishments and your potential for good.

Inside this book is everything you need to know about Auradon: places to see, people to meet, classes to take, and tips and secrets for making the most of your time here. We've even included space for you to add your own advice for future students on how to put together a winning essay and application.

Since I arrived at Auradon Prep, everything in my life has changed. I have my own business, I bought my own starter castle, and I've met someone who is really special. But even on my best days in Auradon, I never forget about the world I left behind.

There are so many kids on the Isle who aren't as lucky as I have been. I've always thought there must be a way to bring them to Auradon and give them the same chances I've been given. I want their lives to change the same way mine has. That's why I got King Ben to agree to bring more villain kids to Auradon Prep.

King Ben started the program with us, the first four VKs, and then said I could expand it as a mentoring program and bring more VKs over. We only had four spots to fill and so many applications from the Isle. Maybe one day more Isle of the Lost kids will be invited to Auradon. At least that's my hope. For now, this is your chance for something better . . . to make your life good.

I hope you will take this opportunity and change your life starting today!

I hope so too, Evie.
BUT FOR NOW:
we're so glad you're here!

-Evie

-Mal

AND IF YOU NEED ANYTHING—SERIOUSLY ANYTHING—COME FIND ME AND DUDE. WE'RE ALWAYS IN THE BOYS' DORM, IF YOU WANT ADVICE OR JUST SOMEONE TO TALK TO.

-CARLOS

COME ON, WE NEED TO PUT THE WELCOME IN THIS WELCOME PACKET. WHY'S EVERYONE SO SERIOUS?

IF YOU'RE READING THIS . . .

YOU MADE IT TO AURADON! YOU WERE ONE OF THE CHOSEN FEW!!

HOW COOL IS THAT?!? GET READY TO ~~PARTY~~!

Enjoy everything Auradon Prep has to offer!

-JAY

Dizzy Tremaine!
(Lady Tremaine's granddaughter)

- Claudine Frollo
(daughter of Judge Claude Frollo)

Eddie Balthazar
(son of Edgar Balthazar)

⭑ Celia Facilier (Dr. Facilier's daughter)

- Yzla
(Yzma's daughter)

Jace and Harry Badun
(the sons of Cruella De Vil's henchmen)

- Squeaky and Squirmy
(Smee's sons)

This is where it all STARTED—EVIE'S big idea. She made this list a while ago and gave it to Ben for consideration. IT'S all the villain kids who she thought deserved a chance at Auradon Prep, and a few who she really felt NEEDED it.

I REMEMBER THESE TWO. I HEARD THAT AFTER MAL'S MOM WAS DEFEATED, THEY JOINED THIS SECRET ORGANIZATION THE WIZARD YEN SID FOUNDED. IT'S CALLED THE ANTI-HEROES CLUB. IT'S FOR VILLAIN KIDS WHO ARE DRAWN TO GOOD MORE THAN EVIL. (THE NAME HAS A DOUBLE MEANING, SINCE AN ANTI-HERO FIGHTS FOR GOOD, USING TACTICS A VILLAIN WOULD TO GET THE JOB DONE.)

Evie wasn't sure how many kids Ben would be able to bring to Auradon Prep, so she wrote a short list. But leading up to the big announcement, we were buried in applications. I've never had to go through so much paper in my life. It was like everywhere I turned there was another photo of some doe-eyed Isle of the Lost kid. When we got to the Isle for VK Day (the day we were going to announce who would be admitted to Auradon Prep), there were even more VKs shoving essays and forms into our hands. It reminded me of the day Ben invited us to come to Auradon Prep. But for me, personally, it couldn't have been more different. . . .

The only reason my mom even considered letting me come to Auradon was because she knew it would be an opportunity for evil. I would be the one to get Fairy Godmother's wand and bring down the barrier once and for all. I can only imagine what she would've said if I really did want to go simply to be better, to have a good life. She would've just cackled and told me to go back to my lair.

All of you took such risks to apply. You had to get permission from parents who've been practicing villainy for ages. And not only did you fill out a whole application (I would not have done that), you were all so thoughtful when you wrote your essays or talked about why you wanted to come. I guess what I'm trying to say is . . . not much impresses me, but that does.

WOW. I THINK MAL JUST GAVE OUT A COMPLIMENT!

Be nice, Jay!
Besides, we've got so much to tell you still.
Officially . . .

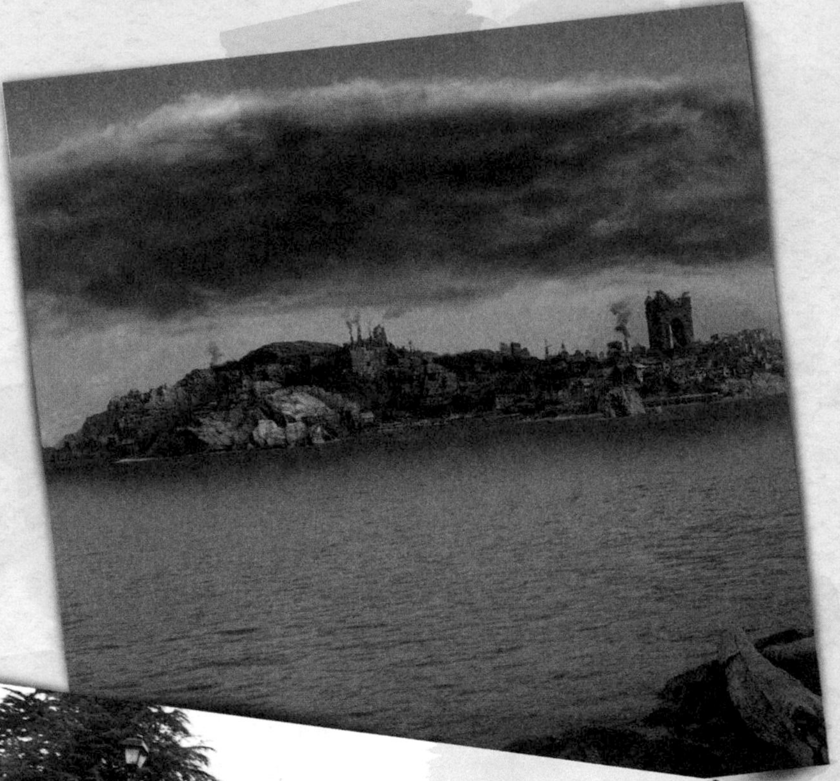

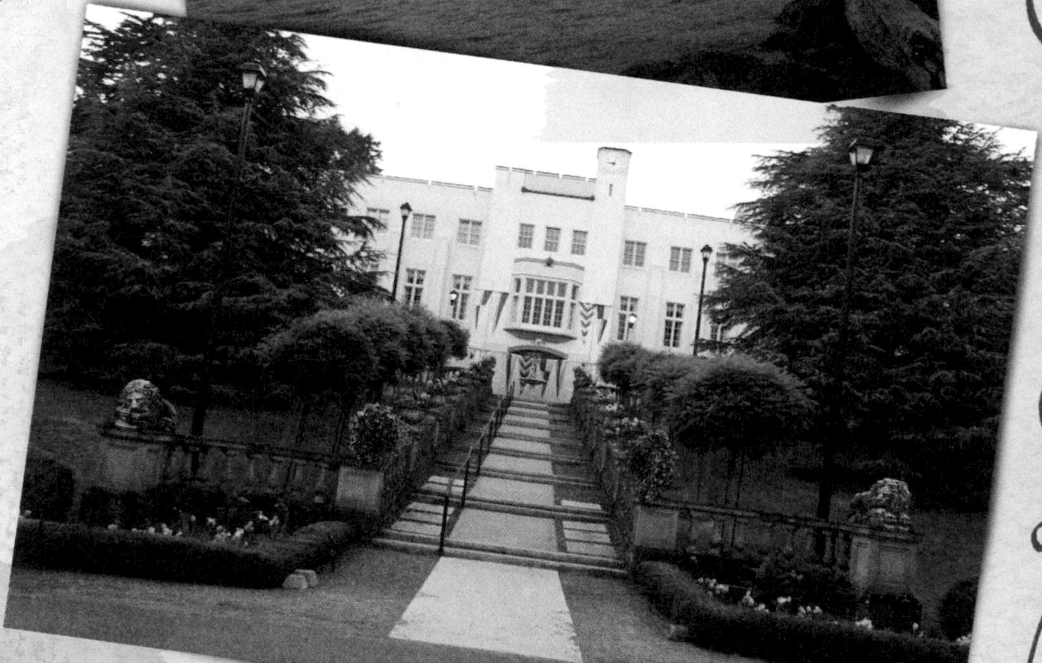

The United States of Auradon

(The USA)

So you've probably heard the history of Auradon at some point over the years. Most kids on the Isle of the Lost have. They'll tell you how horrible Beast and Belle are. They'll tell you that uniting the fairy-tale kingdoms was the biggest mistake ever made—the beginning of the end. There are reasons for the villains to be angry, of course. They were banished to the Isle of the Lost, a place where their magic no longer works. And with a magic barrier in place, they've had no choice but to call the Isle home.

But on the Isle, they don't tell you all the ways that Auradon has prospered under Beast and Belle's rule. Beast gave the United States of Auradon the greatest gift any king has ever given his kingdom. Peace. Not having to worry, ever, about enemies or evil. Knowing you're safe. It's a special thing.

I MEAN, I DEFINITELY HEARD THE STORY HUNDREDS OF TIMES FROM MY MOM. TWENTY YEARS AGO, INSTEAD OF DOING WHAT EVERY OTHER NORMAL MARRIED COUPLE DOES AND GOING TO THE SUMMERLANDS FOR A WEEKLONG HONEYMOON, KING BEAST AND BELLE DECIDED TO ROUND UP ALL THE VILLAINS AND PUT THEM ON THE ISLE OF THE LOST. THEN THE KING REALLY WENT TO WORK, UNITING ALL THE FAIRY-TALE KINGDOMS INTO THE UNITED STATES OF AURADON AND

RULING THAT MAGIC WAS NOW FORBIDDEN. HE WANTED KIDS GROWING UP IN AURADON TO RELY ON THEIR OWN TALENTS AND SKILLS, SO HE PUT FAIRY GODMOTHER IN CHARGE OF ENFORCING THE "NO MORE MAGIC" RULE. BESIDES, WITHOUT VILLAINS, NONE OF THE HEROES OR THEIR CHILDREN NEEDED MAGIC TO DEFEND THEMSELVES. THEY WERE SAFE.

IT WAS A GOOD PLAN, EXCEPT FOR THE BANISH-OUR-FAMILIES-TO-A-HORRIBLE-ISLAND PART. THE MAGIC BARRIER MAKES IT FEEL LIKE ONE BIG PRISON, WITH EVERYONE TRAPPED INSIDE.

I GUESS THEY WEREN'T SURE WHAT TO DO WITH US. SOMETIMES I WONDER IF YOU CAN REALLY BLAME THEM . . . WE WERE BAD. EVIL. PLAIN AND SIMPLE . . .

AND THE REALITY IS, WHATEVER THEY DID WORKED. AURADON IS SAFE NOW. PEOPLE ARE HAPPY AND CAREFREE. THAT'S NOT WHAT IT'S LIKE ON THE ISLE.

I almost didn't want to write about this, because we could argue about it for days. Let's just move on. There are so many things to do and see in the USA. We hardly have time to list all of them, but we'll try. . . .

Places to See

Auradon Cathedral

You probably know all about Auradon Cathedral already, especially if you watch the Auradon News Network. This is where all the famous heroes have been married, christened, or crowned. The stained glass windows have pictures of Snow White, Belle and the Beast, Cinderella, Ariel, Aurora, and Mulan (and many, many others). But you probably remember hearing about it because it was where one of the greatest battles in Auradon took place. It was there that Mal defeated her mom, Maleficent, and saved all of Auradon.

TRUE STORY. I TURNED MY OWN MOTHER INTO a liZaRd.

The Enchanted Lake

This lake is north of Auradon Prep in the middle of a beautiful forest. It's always been one of my favorite places in Auradon, and not just because Ben and I had our first date there, right by the stone pillar. The water is this really incredible jade color, and there are tons of trees and flowers. It's quiet and beautiful—in other words, the complete opposite of the Isle. It's the perfect place to relax, or you can bring some snacks and picnic there.

And, as I mentioned, it's also where Ben and I had our first date.

THE WATER IS KNOWN FOR WASHING AWAY SPELLS AND ENCHANTMENTS. LIKE, FOR EXAMPLE, IF SOMEONE SPELLED YOU TO FALL IN LOVE WITH THEM, YOU COULD JUMP INTO THE LAKE AND BE RESTORED TO YOUR OLD SELF. THEN YOU COULD DECIDE HOW YOU REALLY FEEL ABOUT THE PURPLE ONE.

VERY FUNNY, Jay.

MUSEUM OF CULTURAL HISTORY

THE FIRST TIME I WENT HERE WAS PRETTY MEMORABLE. I ACCIDENTALLY SET OFF THE ALARM, AND WE HAD TO SPRINT THROUGH THE WOODS SO WE WOULDN'T GET CAUGHT BY THE GUARDS. BUT THINGS ARE DIFFERENT NOW, AND EVEN THOUGH I'M NOT CRAZY ABOUT THE AURADON PREP FIELD TRIPS TO THE MUSEUM, I'LL ADMIT IT'S PRETTY COOL TO SEE ALL THE OBJECTS THAT ARE IN THERE.

They have almost every magical object you could think of (including my magic mirror): King Triton's trident, Cinderella's glass slipper, Maleficent's scepter, the enchanted rose, Fairy Godmother's magic wand, Aladdin's magic lamp and magic carpet, the spinning wheel, and Mal's spell book. **UGH, DON'T REMIND ME.**

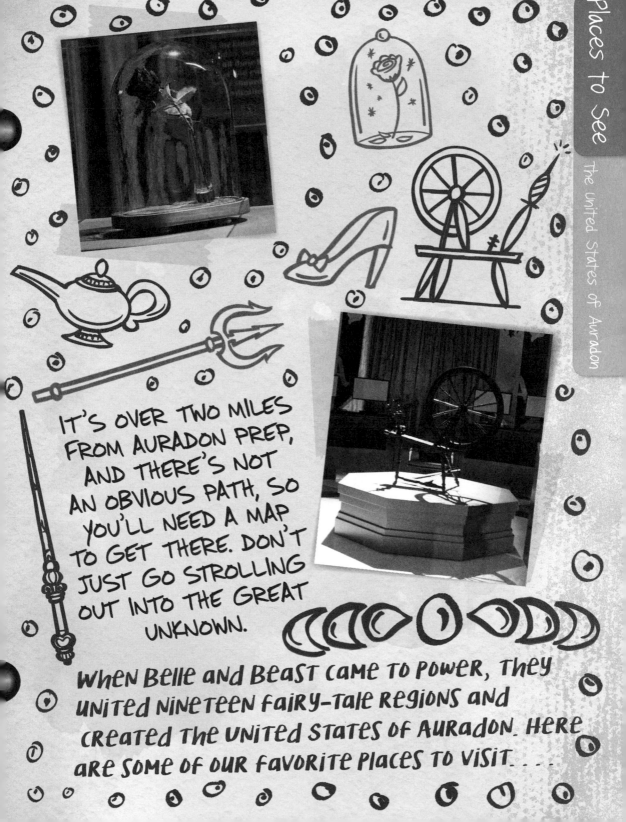

IT'S OVER TWO MILES FROM AURADON PREP, AND THERE'S NOT AN OBVIOUS PATH, SO YOU'LL NEED A MAP TO GET THERE. DON'T JUST GO STROLLING OUT INTO THE GREAT UNKNOWN.

WHEN BELLE AND BEAST CAME TO POWER, THEY UNITED NINETEEN FAIRY-TALE REGIONS AND CREATED THE UNITED STATES OF AURADON. HERE ARE SOME OF OUR FAVORITE PLACES TO VISIT. . . . .

Agrabah

The Great Wall of Auradon

Triton's Bay

Lone Keep

Camelot Heights

Sherwood Forest

Enchanted Lake

Charmington

Bel Har

Cinderellasburg

N

E

W

S

Isle of the Lost

Skull Rock

Never Land

Mount Olympus

Summerlands

Hook's Bay

Museum of Cultural History

Rapunzel's Tower

Auradon Cathedral

Auradon City

Bayou De Orleans

Auroria

The United States of Auradon

WONDERLAND

THE ONLY WAY TO FIND THIS
PLACE IS TO FIND THE WHITE
RABBIT FIRST. HE'LL TAKE YOU
DOWN THE RABBIT HOLE INTO
THIS UPSIDE-DOWN, COLORFUL
WORLD. I'VE NEVER BEEN, BUT IF
YOU MAKE IT THERE YOU HAVE
TO TELL ME HOW IT IS. I HEARD
THEY SERVE THE BEST TEA AND
CRUMPETS IN AURADON (IF YOU
CAN STAND THE RIDDLES).

Olympus

Mount Olympus, or Olympus for short, is where Hercules and the rest of the gods live. You can see it from nearly everywhere in Auradon—it's that stone building high above, off to the northeast. It's entirely made of clouds except for the pillars in the center. You'll know Olympians because they're always going on about how "otherworldly" and "godly" they are.

I HATE PLAYING THE OLYMPIANS IN TOURNEY. NOT ONLY ARE THEY FULL OF THEMSELVES, BUT THEIR BICEPS ARE THE SIZE OF MY HEAD.

CAMELOT HEIGHTS

I COULDN'T SURVIVE IN CAMELOT HEIGHTS. KING ARTHUR, GUINEVERE, AND SIR LANCELOT AREN'T INTO TECHNOLOGY. IT'S LIKE LIVING IN THE DARK AGES, WITH NO MAGIC TO LIVEN THINGS UP, EITHER.

When Doug and I went there to pick up this dyed wool I really love, the Knights of the Round Table were having a jousting tournament. It's not really my thing, but Jay would have loved it.

I THINK MERLIN LIVES THERE, RIGHT? I WOULDN'T GO, BUT I'LL ADMIT THE TWO CASTLES ARE COOL. CAMELOT CASTLE AND PENDRAGON CASTLE. YOU CAN SEE THEM FROM THE AURADON CITY BORDER.

CINDERELLASBURG

I WANTED TO NOT LIKE CINDERELLASBURG, JUST BECAUSE IT'S WHERE CHAD CHARMING GREW UP. BUT IT REALLY IS ONE OF THE COOLEST PLACES TO SEE. THE MAIN CITY, CERENTOLA, IS SO CLEAN IT SPARKLES. SOME OF THE TOWN'S MICE AND BIRDS SPEND THEIR DAYS POLISHING AND SWEEPING THE STREETS, ALL IN HONOR OF CINDERELLA. YOU CAN SEE YOUR REFLECTION IN THE WALL OUTSIDE ROCKY POINT COURT.

I know, it's so beautiful there. Prince Charming's castle is one of my favorites in Auradon. I love the pink stone walls and the turquoise roof.

CHARMINGTON

DON'T LET ITS NAME FOOL YOU—PRINCE CHARMING DOESN'T LIVE HERE. THIS IS ACTUALLY WHERE SNOW WHITE AND PRINCE FLORIAN'S CASTLE IS. PRINCE FLORIAN, WHO WAS ORIGINALLY KNOWN FOR HIS CHARM AND GOOD LOOKS BEFORE PRINCE CHARMING CAME ON THE SCENE, GREW UP HERE. IT'S HARD TO COMPETE WITH A NAME LIKE PRINCE CHARMING.

I kind of love this place, and not just because it's where Doug's family is from. His uncles are some of the greatest people I've ever met. In fact, everyone in this region is incredible. People are so warm and welcoming that it always feels like you're coming home, even if it's not actually your home. Does that make sense?

TOTALLY. IT'S CLOSE TO THE BORDER OF AURADON CITY, SO I TOOK JANE THERE ONCE FOR DINNER. I THOUGHT SHE WENT THERE ALL THE TIME BECAUSE EVERYONE KEPT SAYING HI TO HER AND WAVING, BUT IT TURNS OUT PEOPLE THERE ARE JUST REALLY, REALLY NICE. DUDE MUST'VE GOTTEN LIKE TEN DIFFERENT TREATS—INCLUDING A HUGE BONE. EVERYONE WAS STOPPING TO PET HIM.

NEVER LAND

OKAY, SO WHAT BOY DOESN'T WANT TO JUST HANG OUT WITH HIS FRIENDS FOR THE REST OF HIS LIFE, PLAYING GAMES AND JOKING AROUND? WHO REALLY WANTS TO GROW UP? I ALWAYS KIND OF LOVE GOING TO NEVER LAND, EVEN IF YOU CAN'T FLY THERE LIKE YOU USED TO. IT'S JUST SO MUCH FUN. THE LOST BOYS ARE STILL WILD AFTER ALL THESE YEARS. WALK INTO ANY RESTAURANT AND YOU'LL PROBABLY BE DRAWN INTO A FOOD FIGHT OR A CARD GAME. THEY ALWAYS WANT TO MAKE NEW FRIENDS.

<u>Ugh</u>! The Lost Boys are <u>SO annoying</u>! I do love going to Mermaid Lagoon, though. It's really peaceful there. Doug took me there, and we sat and watched the mermaids glide through the water, their iridescent tails glittering in the sun. They can be a bit mischievous, so just don't get too close (unless you like getting seaweed in your hair).

SHERWOOD FOREST

SHERWOOD FOREST IS ABOUT SIX HOURS AWAY FROM AURADON CITY. IT'S IN WESTERLY—ONE OF THE NINETEEN REGIONS OF AURADON. WE PLAYED TOURNEY AGAINST THE SHERWOOD FALCONS ONCE. I DON'T KNOW HOW TO DESCRIBE IT ... EXCEPT IT'S KIND OF EXACTLY LIKE YOU'D THINK IT WOULD BE. TONS OF TREES, EVERYTHING'S REALLY GREEN. BEFORE WE CAME BACK, WE ATE DINNER AT THIS CAFÉ CALLED THE MERRY MEN. IT'S IN LOCKSLEY, ROBIN HOOD'S HOMETOWN, AND THEY SERVED REALLY GREAT STEW THERE. THE COOLEST PART IS THAT EVERYTHING ON THE MENU IS FREE—THEY WANT EVERYONE TO BE ABLE TO ENJOY THE FOOD THERE, NO MATTER HOW RICH OR POOR YOU ARE.

Belle's Harbor

Some of my best memories are at Belle's Harbor. Ben's family owns this speedboat called <u>Beast's Fury</u>, and Ben and I went out on it once right at sunset. We were whipping around the harbor, kicking up waves and going so fast I had to hold on to the railing. It was strange to be between the Isle of the Lost and Auradon—my past and my future. It's like parts of me live in both.

AURORIA

TOO MUCH HISTORY THERE! EVIE, YOU GOT THIS ONE?

I've been there to buy tulle. It's a city in South Riding, to the southeast of Auradon City, and it has lots of cute shops and cafés. Goodly Point has a famous restaurant called The Briar Rose. They only serve dessert, and all the food and drinks are fit for a princess: chocolate-covered strawberries, sparkling cider, vanilla custard, and blueberry tarts. If you go there, definitely try their macarons.

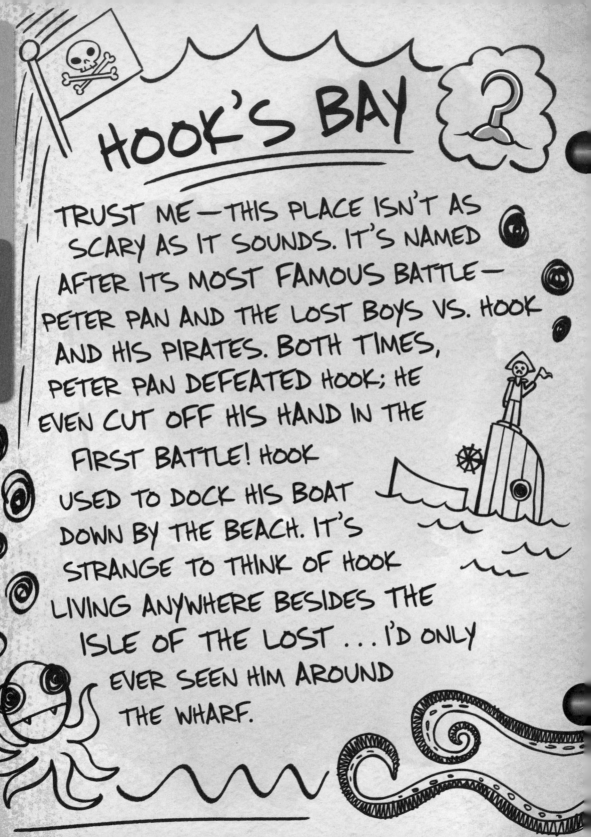

HOOK'S BAY

TRUST ME—THIS PLACE ISN'T AS SCARY AS IT SOUNDS. IT'S NAMED AFTER ITS MOST FAMOUS BATTLE— PETER PAN AND THE LOST BOYS VS. HOOK AND HIS PIRATES. BOTH TIMES, PETER PAN DEFEATED HOOK; HE EVEN CUT OFF HIS HAND IN THE FIRST BATTLE! HOOK USED TO DOCK HIS BOAT DOWN BY THE BEACH. IT'S STRANGE TO THINK OF HOOK LIVING ANYWHERE BESIDES THE ISLE OF THE LOST . . . I'D ONLY EVER SEEN HIM AROUND THE WHARF.

TRITON'S Bay

I CAN ONly Tell you The RUMORS about TRITON'S Bay, because I'VE NEVER been There Myself. IT'S a full week's journey FROM AURADON CITY. MOST STUDENTS ONly go ON SPRING break OR during the Summer (if they go at all). The beaches have Some of the best dance clubs in all of AURADON. Kids Stay up late listening to Music and hanging out. I heard there's a Really cool water park Nearby with CRAZY fast Slides and amazing CHURROS. YUM!

AGRABAH

I'VE NEVER BEEN, BUT I'VE HEARD SO MANY STORIES ABOUT AGRABAH FROM MY DAD. HE EVEN HAD THIS PICTURE OF THE PLACE ABOVE HIS DESK AT THE JUNK SHOP. I MUST'VE STARED AT THAT PHOTO A HUNDRED TIMES, IMAGINING WHAT IT WOULD BE LIKE TO GROW UP THERE.

IT'S IN A DESERT BEYOND THE GREAT WALL OF AURADON, RISING UP FROM THE SAND LIKE A MIRAGE. AGRABAH LOOKS LIKE IT'S MADE OF GOLD. THE BUILDINGS AND ROOFTOPS ARE ALL THIS ORANGE-ISH SAND COLOR, WITH PURPLE AWNINGS BREAKING UP THE LANDSCAPE. ALADDIN AND JASMINE STILL LIVE IN THE SULTAN'S PALACE, THOUGH THEY COME INTO AURADON CITY EVERY NOW AND THEN.

💀 Skull Rock

This is the place captain Hook and Smee took Tiger Lily after they captured her. It's abandoned now, and all the crocodiles have left for the Isle of the Lost. Some of the Bayou kids take boats out there and hang out inside the skull's hollow eyes. Sometimes you can see their silhouettes from the beach or hear their laughs echoing over the bay.

Summerlands

This place is seriously one of the highlights of coming to Auradon. The royals spend whole summers at the resorts here, which are perfect for swimming, hiking, kayaking, bicycle riding, and pretty much any other happy-making activity you can think of. I've only been to Summerlands once, with Doug, and we went to this beautiful park with waterfalls. I'd never actually seen one before.

DUDE AND I TOOK A DAY TRIP HERE MY FIRST YEAR IN AURADON. WE HIKED THREE MILES! I'D NEVER SEEN TREES THAT GREEN BEFORE.

They say it's the land of fairy tales. A lot of what happened to Snow White and Sleeping Beauty took place here.

Summer in Summerlands

Paradise Awaits You

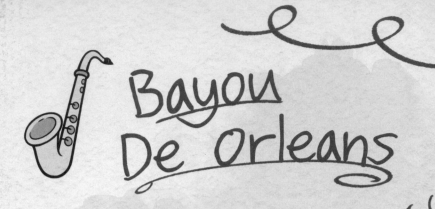

Bayou De Orleans

This city has some of the best food you can find in Auradon. Beignets, fried shrimp, crawfish, and jambalaya. If you're a music lover, definitely check out some of the bands here. There are dozens of great jazz clubs right on the water (and great fashion, too—I love that Bayou style).

TIANA AND NAVEEN LIVE HERE—THEY'RE TWO OF MY FAVORITE HEROES.

Rapunzel's Tower

Good luck finding this place. It doesn't matter how clearly it's marked on all the Auradon maps, give yourself an extra two hours to get there. The tower was built in a rock quarry, but you have to go through the forest, and then a hidden cave, just to get there. You can stroll around and see all the different murals Rapunzel painted while she was captive. My favorites have always been the astronomical paintings. There's one of the solar system, with Corona's symbolic sun at the center, and another that's a star map so you can locate all the different constellations.

The BEST of AURadoN City

The heart of Auradon is Auradon City, with its narrow streets and cute little shops and cafés. The main drag is just a five-minute walk from Auradon Prep's quad, so this is where we go when we want to have an off-campus adventure. There are tons of great places to explore. I'm biased, but one of my favorites is Culinary Cabaret. It's this great restaurant on Main Street that has all the different treats Lumiere, Cogsworth, Mrs. Potts, and the castle dishes served Belle when she first arrived at Beast's Castle. Try the grey stuff (obviously) and the French onion soup.

Just be warned: you actually have to shout, "ENOUGH, I'M DONE!" to get them to stop bringing you food. Those candlesticks will stuff you like a Cornish hen.

Culinary Cabaret

If you're stressed, it's fine dining we suggest.

Beef Ragout

Cheese Soufflé

Pie
blackberry, pecan, unpoisoned apple

Pudding en Flambé

Soup du Jour
French onion

The Grey Stuff

Tea
herbal, lemon verbena, Mrs. Potts's favorite
choice of sugar, one lump or two

The Queen's Closet

This consignment store is a diamond in the rough. What's consignment, you ask? Royals from all over Auradon bring their gently used ball gowns and dresses here to resell them. Capes and tiaras, clutches and elbow-length gloves—they have it all. It reminded me of the Isle of the Lost a little at first, just in the way we were always expected to want leftovers from Auradon. But these aren't leftovers, not really. They're truly beautiful items that barely have any wear and tear. Mal wasn't crazy about this, but I found a great pink scarf that used to belong to Aurora. I turned it into a sash for one of my Evie's 4 Hearts couture ball gowns.

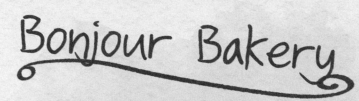

Bonjour Bakery

At the end of Main Street, just two doors down from the Queen's Closet, is this tiny bakery. You can find it by following the scent of freshly baked bread (if you'd told me three years ago that I'd grow to love the smell of freshly baked bread, I would not have believed you). This place sells croissants, baguettes, fresh eggs, and pastries. Pretty much everything on their menu is buttery and delicious.

Belle likes to go there because it reminds her of the bakery where she used to hang out in her hometown.

BEYOND THE DRAGON FIRE

I COULD SPEND WEEKS IN THIS STORE. IT'S DOWN A SIDE STREET CALLED RIQUEWIHR, AND IT HAS EVERYTHING YOU NEED IF YOU'RE GOING TO PLAY TOURNEY FOR AURADON PREP: HELMETS, STICKS, BODY ARMOR, SPIKED CLEATS, TOURNEY BALLS, GLOVES, SHORTS, AND UNIFORMS. YOU CAN EVEN GET ONE OF THE STURDIEST SHIELDS AVAILABLE HERE—IT'S PROTECTED ME FROM SOME POWERFUL BLASTS OF DRAGON FIRE.

AND IF YOU DO GET HIT, THEY HAVE SOME GREAT BALM FOR DRAGON FIRE BURNS. PUT IT ON YOUR SKIN AND YOU'LL BE BACK TO NORMAL IN TWO DAYS . . . THREE TOPS.

The Candlestick Café

This is a great spot to hang out after school, or if you're looking for a quiet place off campus to study. They let you sit and read at their tables for hours without bothering you. They mainly serve tea and biscuits, but sometimes they'll make hot cocoa for you if you ask nicely. (Auradon pro tip: people will do a lot of things if you just ask nicely.)

BEAST'S CASTLE

I KNOW MAL'S BEEN HERE A THOUSAND TIMES, AND IT'S PROBABLY NOT A BIG DEAL TO HER, BUT I LOVE GOING ON TOURS THROUGH BEAST'S CASTLE. ONE WHOLE SECTION IS STILL OPEN TO THE PUBLIC. IT EVEN INCLUDES A WALK THROUGH THE FORBIDDEN WEST WING. THEY'VE RESTORED MOST OF IT, BUT LEFT SOME OF THE CLAW MARKS AND BROKEN DOORS IN HONOR OF THE BEAST'S LOST YEARS. IT REALLY DOES HAVE A CREEPY FEEL COMPARED TO THE REST OF THE CASTLE.

THE WEST WING IS AWESOME! I LOVE WHEN THEY TAKE YOU TO THE WOODS OUTSIDE THE CASTLE, AND YOU CAN SEE THE SPOT WHERE BEAST FOUGHT THAT PACK OF WOLVES. I MEAN, I'M GLAD EVERYTHING'S BACK TO NORMAL FOR HIM, BUT THAT MUST HAVE BEEN A COOL SUPERPOWER.

I NEVER THOUGHT I'd Say THIS, BUT MY FAVORITE ROOM has always BEEN THE LIBRARY. THEY CLOSED IT TO THE PUBLIC YEARS ago, BUT BEN TOOK ME IN TO SEE THE SHELVES and SHELVES of LEATHER-BOUND BOOKS. IT'S INCREDIBLY ROMANTIC, THINKING ABOUT HIS dad GIVING THAT LIBRARY TO HIS MOM.

LOOK HOW YOUNG BEN IS IN THE PORTRAIT!

Who's Who of Auradon

Many of these heroes you've heard about from your years on the Isle of the Lost. But it's very possible you'll run into them in Auradon City, or hear them speak at one of Auradon Prep's assemblies. Here's a quick guide to all the biggest names in the USA.

(KING) BEN

What can I say about Ben? King Benjamin Florian Beast, if you want to get specific. He's the reason I'm in Auradon in the first place—he literally changed my life . . . or to be more accurate, all our lives! If he hadn't gazed out the window that day and decided we VKs deserved a chance, I'd still be in my mother's house, listening to her blather on about that christening she wasn't invited to. He's kind and gentle and sees the best in everyone, including every kid from the Isle. He'll be the first one to defend you at Auradon Prep, and he'll never give up on you. He's one of the most optimistic people I know.

HE HELPED ME SO MUCH WHEN I GOT HERE. HE TRAINED ME FOR THE TOURNEY TEAM AND INTRODUCED ME TO DUDE, THE CAMPUS MUTT, WHO DIDN'T ACTUALLY WANT TO RIP MY THROAT OUT.

THE GUY'S A <u>GOOD</u> PERSON, PLAIN AND SIMPLE. MAYBE THE BEST I'VE EVER MET.

I mean, he agreed to bring more VKs to Auradon AND he treats my best friend like gold. No complaints here.

YEAH, I LIKE THE GUY, AND I DON'T LIKE MANY PEOPLE (REALLY <u>SERIOUSLY</u> LIKE THEM) SO THAT MEANS A LOT.

Belle

The former queen of Auradon is one of the kindest people you'll ever meet. She's beautiful inside and out, and she always looks for the best in people. When her son, Ben, told her he wanted to give Isle of the Lost kids a chance at Auradon Prep, she supported him, even though she was worried about what it would mean for the kingdom. She's been like a mother to me, now that I'm on my own.

BeaST

I know Ben's dad was once an arrogant, mean prince, but you'd never know that if you met him today. Those years living as the beast really transformed him into someone humble and kind. He still has a bit of a temper (I don't think that will ever go away, even though his fur and tail have) but overall he's a really nice guy. He supported Ben's bringing the original VKs over, even though it was hard. And when Ben was spelled by Uma and presented her at Cotillion, Beast was the one who tried to comfort me. I can still see his face. He was so sad that Ben had done that to me. He just wanted to make everything better.

WE SHOULDN'T TALK ABOUT THAT NIGHT. I KNOW BEN WAS UNDER A LOVE SPELL, BUT IT STILL MAKES ME ANGRY.

FAIRY GODMOTHER

JANE'S MOM IS RAD. SERIOUSLY. A LOT OF AURADON PREP STUDENTS THINK SHE'S A BIT STIFF OR TOO CONCERNED WITH GOODNESS AND MANNERS, BUT NOW THAT I KNOW HER I UNDERSTAND WHERE SHE'S COMING FROM. AS THE HEADMISTRESS OF AURADON PREP, SHE'S THE ONE RESPONSIBLE FOR TEACHING AURADON KIDS HOW TO USE THEIR TALENTS AND SKILLS INSTEAD OF RELYING ON MAGIC. SHE ENCOURAGES US TO LEARN AND GROW, TO READ AS MUCH AS POSSIBLE, AND TO CHOOSE GOOD—ALWAYS. SHE FOLLOWS THE RULES, AND SHE WANTS US TO FOLLOW THEM, TOO. THAT'S HER JOB. I MEAN, SHE'S REALLY NICE ABOUT IT, RIGHT?

Definitely.
She's one of the nicest heroes I've ever met.

COACH JENKINS

I OWE COACH JENKINS EVERYTHING. WHEN I FIRST GOT TO AURADON PREP I WAS A LITTLE LOST, AND HE SAW THAT I HAD RAW TALENT FOR TOURNEY. I SPENT MY YEARS ON THE ISLE PLAYING STICK BALL IN THE ALLEY BEHIND FROLLO'S CREPERIE, AND IT REALLY PAID OFF. I COULD RUN JUST AS FAST, IF NOT FASTER, THAN MOST OF THE GUYS ON THE TEAM. I COULD EXECUTE COMPLICATED MOVES. SURE, I DIDN'T KNOW ANYTHING ABOUT TEAMWORK OR THAT MAYBE YOU SHOULDN'T CHECK SOMEONE SO HARD THAT THEY CAN'T GET UP FOR TEN MINUTES AFTERWARD. BUT COACH JENKINS TAUGHT ME HOW TO PLAY THE RIGHT WAY. HE SHOWED ME THAT THE TEAM IS STRONGER TOGETHER THAN ANY OF US PLAYERS ARE ON OUR OWN.

YOU'RE FORGETTING HOW HE LET ME PLAY IN THE TOURNAMENT, EVEN THOUGH I WAS ABOUT HALF THE SIZE OF THE OTHER KIDS AND TERRIFIED OF DRAGON FIRE. HE GAVE ME A CHANCE TO PROVE MYSELF.

YOU DIDN'T JUST PROVE YOURSELF, YOU ACED IT. YOU LOOKED LIKE YOU'D BEEN PLAYING TOURNEY FOR YEARS.

We don't have any good pictures of Mr. Deley. But, that's him, lurking in the background.

Mr. Deley

It might take a while to get your footing at Auradon Prep, so beware of Mr. Deley. He's a stickler for the rules, and he's always looking for any excuse to send a villain kid back to the Isle. I used my magic mirror a couple of times to help me through chemistry class but then Mr. Deley found out. If it weren't for Doug standing up for me, I probably would've gotten expelled.

DUDE

MAYBE MOST DOGS DON'T NEED A FORMAL INTRODUCTION, BUT DUDE ISN'T MOST DOGS. HE WAS THE AURADON PREP CAMPUS MUTT WHEN WE CAME HERE, AND BEN USED HIM TO TRAIN ME OUT OF MY PHOBIA OF DOGS. IT'S JUST THAT GROWING UP, MY MOM TAUGHT ME ALL DOGS WERE VICIOUS BEASTS THAT WOULD RIP ME APART THE FIRST CHANCE THEY GOT. BUT WHEN DUDE AND I FINALLY DID MEET, HE WAS ALL SWEETNESS AND LOVE. HE'S BECOME MY BEST FRIEND.

I'LL TRY NOT TO TAKE THAT PERSONALLY.

But also: You're forgetting the BEST part. Ever since Dude ate one of Mal's magic truth serum gummies, he's been able to talk. If you run into him on campus, don't be alarmed if he asks you to scratch his butt.

Chad

Chad is not a big fan of anyone from the Isle, so he's not going to be your best friend. When I first came to Auradon, I had a crush on him, but looking back, I think I'd just been brainwashed by all the fairy tales about Prince Charming. He might be Cinderella's son, but the truth is he's not as kind as his mother. He DOES have good fashion taste, though. I created his outfit for Cotillion, and he actually agreed to let me put faux fur on the collar.

I'VE HAD MY RUN-INS WITH THIS GUY, BUT I HAVE TO ADMIT, HE'S A GREAT TOURNEY PLAYER.

Doug

aka my favorite person
(besides you Mal) :)

There's so much to like about Doug. He's sweet, kind, smart, a little shy, and the best accountant a small business could have. He's Dopey's son, and even though my mom has a long history with his family, he never treated me differently because of that. When Chad tried to get me kicked out of school, Doug was the one who stood up for me with Mr. Deley. If you ever need an Auradon student to go to for advice, or to tutor you in science or math—Doug is your guy. He was the one who showed us around those first weeks of school.

Oh! I didn't even mention how talented he is. He plays trumpet in the Auradon Prep marching band and wants to play with the Dragon Slayers one day. It's this rock band that performs in clubs around Auradon City.

LONNIE

LONNIE IS ONE OF THE COOLEST GIRLS AT AURADON PREP. SHE'S FA MULAN AND LI SHANG'S DAUGHTER, SO SHE HAS INCREDIBLE SWORD-FIGHTING SKILLS. WHEN SHE HEARD BEN HAD BEEN CAPTURED ON THE ISLE, SHE DEMANDED THAT CARLOS AND JAY TAKE HER ACROSS THE BARRIER WITH THEM TO FIGHT. HAVING HER THERE WHEN WE BATTLED UMA'S PIRATES SAVED US. NOT MANY HEROES WOULD VOLUNTEER TO GO TO THE ISLE OF THE LOST. THAT WAS CRAZY BRAVE.

SHE'S ALSO THE CAPTAIN OF THE SWORDS AND SHIELDS TEAM. NO ONE IS BETTER AT STRIKING OR BOSSING AROUND EIGHT GUYS.

JANE

JANE IS FAIRY GODMOTHER'S DAUGHTER. SHE'S SWEET AND KIND, AND SHE ALWAYS GOES OUT OF HER WAY TO HELP OTHERS. SHE'S KNOWN FOR PLANNING THE GREATEST PARTIES AURADON PREP HAS EVER SEEN.

I WAS REALLY NERVOUS THE HEADMISTRESS WOULDN'T APPROVE OF ME. I MEAN, WHO WANTS THEIR DAUGHTER TO GO OUT WITH THE SON OF CRUELLA DE VIL? BUT, AS YOU'LL SEE ONCE YOU ARE HERE IN AURADON FOR A LITTLE WHILE, NOT EVERYONE JUDGES YOU BY WHO YOUR PARENTS ARE.

ANYWAYS, JANE GREW UP HERE AND KNOWS HER WAY AROUND AURADON . . . AND EVERYONE WHO LIVES HERE. SO IF YOU NEED ADVICE ABOUT ANYTHING AND EVERYTHING, SHE'S THE FIRST PERSON I'D TURN TO FOR HELP.

Audrey

Audrey loves being a princess. She was all ready to live her happily ever after with Ben until we arrived. Mal and Ben fell in love, and the rest is history. So, needless to say, Audrey's not a big supporter of the VKs. Maybe I'm wrong, but after everything that happened at Ben's coronation, when Mal saved the kingdom, I don't think she holds a grudge.

Audrey's grandmother Queen Leah does, though. Mal's mom took her daughter away from her for those sixteen years. She's not going to forget it any time soon, no matter how good Mal is or how much she does for the kingdom.

I KNOW MY MOTHER DESTROYED HER FAMILY. IT'S NOT SOMETHING I'M PROUD OF. SOMETIMES I JUST WANT TO TELL AUDREY AND QUEEN LEAH THAT IT WASN'T MY FAULT AND I DON'T HAVE A WAY TO CHANGE THE PAST.

THE COUNCIL OF SIDEKICKS

THESE ARE THE UNSUNG HEROES OF AURADON. I'VE ALWAYS LIKED THAT PHRASE. IT MEANS THEY DO A LOT OF GOOD IN THE WORLD BUT THEY DON'T ALWAYS GET CREDIT FOR IT. SEE, NO ONE TALKS ABOUT LUMIERE AND COGSWORTH SAVING THE KINGDOM, OR HOW THE GENIE SHOULD HAVE HIS OWN PALACE IN AGRABAH. BUT THEY DID, AND THE GENIE SHOULD.

THE COUNCIL OF SIDEKICKS IS A POWERFUL GROUP THAT EVERY AURADON RESIDENT SHOULD KNOW. THESE SIDEKICKS HAVE AIDED HEROES OVER THE YEARS AND DESERVE RESPECT, EVEN THOUGH THEY ARE OFTEN OVERLOOKED. THEY STILL MEET ALL THESE YEARS AFTER THEIR FAIRY TALES TOOK PLACE, AND EVEN THOUGH THERE ISN'T MAGIC ALLOWED IN AURADON, BEAST MAKES AN EXCEPTION FOR THESE GUYS. THEY USE A MAGICAL TRANSLATOR AT THEIR MEETINGS SO THEY CAN COMMUNICATE WITH EACH OTHER, WHETHER THEY'RE MICE, FISH, A GENIE, OR MERMAIDS.

MEMBERS OF
THE COUNCIL OF SIDEKICKS

FLORA, FAUNA, AND MERRYWEATHER

THE GENIE

THE SEVEN DWARFS

PONGO AND PERDITA

FLOUNDER

JAQ, GUS, AND MARY

ARIEL'S SISTERS

What to Bring

If it isn't already obvious, Auradon is VERY different from the Isle of the Lost. The streets are clean, the skies are blue, and everyone smiles and says hello and asks how you are doing. (I know—it's weird. You'll get used to it.) So when you're packing to come here, you should use these tips as a guide.

—Bring something to remind you of home. I designed and made my wicked blue jacket years ago, when Auradon was just a speck across the Strait of Ursula. Wearing it those first months was a cozy reminder of the Isle, and it made me feel like myself even when everything around me was foreign and strange.

THAT'S WHY I BROUGHT MY LUCKY PENNY. I FOUND IT ON THE STREET WHEN I WAS FIVE AND IT HAS ALWAYS BROUGHT ME GOOD LUCK. I KEEP IT IN MY POCKET WHEREVER I GO.

—Soap. This one is BIG. Sure, you can buy it once you get here, but it's better to start those cleanly habits before you set foot on shore. Auradon Prep kids shower and bathe AND brush their teeth. Which reminds me . . .

—Bring a toothbrush, toothpaste, and dental floss. Clean teeth are important, too!

—SUNSCREEN, a SUN hat, OR SUNGLaSSES. OR Maybe all THREE. IF YOU'VE SPENT YOUR whole life ON THE ISle OF THE LOST, YOU'VE NEVER SEEN THE SUN. And when the SUN'S OUT, YOUR SKIN Can GET bURNT like a PanCaKE. JUST a few MINUTES OF EXPOSURE and YOU'll be a RED, CRUSTY MESS.

Make SURE YOU SlaTHER SUNSCREEN all OVER YOUR faCE and hands, and anywhere ElSE THaT THE SUN'S RaYS Can GET TO. THOSE FIRST FEW MONTHS I WORE lONG SlEEVES and lONG PANTS a lOT because THEY PROTECTED MY SKIN.

—BRING WORKOUT CLOTHES. I DIDN'T REALIZE THIS, BUT IN AURADON PEOPLE CHANGE THEIR CLOTHES ALL THE TIME, FOR DIFFERENT REASONS. SO THEY'LL HAVE ONE OUTFIT FOR LUNCH AND ANOTHER OUTFIT FOR DINNER. THEY ALWAYS WEAR DIFFERENT CLOTHES TO PLAY TOURNEY OR FOR GYM CLASS. WORKOUT CLOTHES ARE JUST MORE CASUAL CLOTHES THAT YOU CAN GET DIRTY. OR MAYBE THEY'RE OLD CLOTHES THAT YOU DON'T CARE ABOUT. JUST DON'T WEAR THE SAME THING.

—OH! AND AN OLD RAG AND POLISH TO SHINE YOUR SHOES AND BOOTS. MOST KIDS ON AURADON DON'T HAVE SCUFF MARKS ON THEIR TOES.

—Any blue or yellow clothing you might have. Blue and yellow are Auradon Prep's colors (more on that soon) and students wear these colors at every sporting event. For tourney games, the bleachers are just a sea of blue and yellow.

Which reminds me: Auradon Prep is nothing like Dragon Hall or Serpent Prep. Be prepared to . . .

PUT SOME PREP IN YOUR STEP

The VKs' Guide to Prep School

Auradon Prep 101

Okay, so you know how it wasn't cool on the Isle of the Lost to study, or be smart, or answer correctly when a teacher asked a question? That is NOT how it works at Auradon Prep. Students start thinking about their class schedules weeks before they're finalized, and everyone wants to give themselves the best chance to succeed.

"SUCCESS" WAS NOT A WORD I HEARD GROWING UP . . . ESPECIALLY WHEN IT CAME TO SCHOOL. IT JUST MEANS THAT YOU MAKE A GOAL AND THEN YOU REACH IT. LIKE IF YOU TELL SOMEONE YOU'RE GOING TO GET AN A ON A TEST, THEN YOU ACTUALLY GET THE A (FOR REAL, YOU DON'T EVEN HAVE TO LIE ABOUT IT).

I KNOW, I KNOW, IT'LL TAKE TIME TO GET USED TO.

In terms of teachers and classes, we've had enough semesters at Auradon Prep to provide you some guidance. If you have any trouble putting together your schedule, just find us and we can help. But for now, here's a quick look at some of the classes you can register for at Auradon Prep.

Remedial Goodness 101

with Fairy Godmother

You don't have a choice with this one. Remedial Goodness is mandatory for all transfers from the Isle of the Lost. Don't even think about cutting, either, because Headmistress Fairy Godmother (or FG as we like to call her) can expel you.

FG will quiz you on all these different scenarios, asking which one means "choosing good." Just pick the answer that sounds the least fun.

Life Skills
without Magic
(taught by Merryweather)

This class is just seriously so incredibly booooooring. Like eyes-glazing-over-almost-falling-asleep boooooooring. Who cares about balancing a checkbook when you have a smartphone? Why do I need to know how to boil water or chop carrots when we can eat at the cafeteria whenever we want? And I've had enough etiquette lessons for a dozen people, thank you very much. (See? I'm already so polite.)

The only thing useful was the traffic rules/traveling without magic section. The first time I took my scooter out, I almost crashed it.

HISTORY OF HUNTSMEN and PIRATES

with TINKER BELL

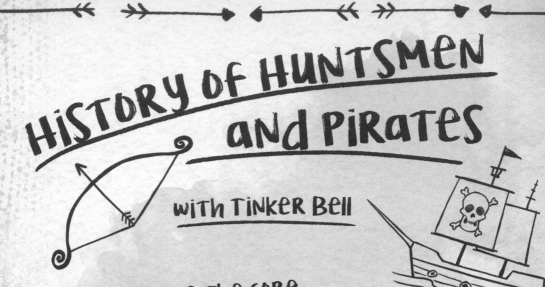

THIS IS PART OF THE CORE CURRICULUM, and I WAS PRETTY obSESSED. SURE, I'VE had a SORDID PAST WITH UMA'S PIRATES, BUT THIS IS MORE about Captain HOOK and SMEE (AS IN YOUR dad, squeaky and squirmy). IT goes THROUGH CENTURIES OF HEROES and VILLAINS SPARRING ON THE OPEN SEAS, and IT also FOLLOWS THE HUNTSMAN WHO WAS HIRED TO go AFTER SNOW WHITE. Basically, IT'S ABOUT VILLAINS, SO IT'S HARD NOT TO RELATE.

THE ONLY PROBLEM WITH THIS CLASS IS THE CLUNKY THINGS YOU HAVE TO WEAR. THEY'RE BIG, HEADPHONES THAT LET YOU HEAR TINKER BELL TALK. HER FAIRY VOICE IS TOO TINY FOR HUMANS TO MAKE OUT OTHERWISE.

MINDFULNESS
WITH MRS. POTTS

THIS ISN'T REALLY A CLASS—IT'S MORE OF AN ELECTIVE THEY MAKE NEW VKS TAKE AFTER SCHOOL. IT'S ALL ABOUT HOW TO ENJOY WHAT'S HAPPENING RIGHT NOW AND LIVE IN THE MOMENT. BECAUSE MRS. POTTS IS ONE OF THE HAPPIEST SIDEKICKS IN AURADON—SHE HAS THESE BIG ROSY CHEEKS THAT MAKE HER LOOK LIKE SHE'S IN A PERMANENT GOOD MOOD—SHE'S THE PERFECT INSTRUCTOR.

IN AURADON, EVERYONE IS INTO SMILING AND BEING MORE POSITIVE. WHAT I DIDN'T REALIZE WAS THAT I'D BEEN SCOWLING MY ENTIRE LIFE. ALL THOSE YEARS ON THE ISLE MEANT I WAS USED TO MAKING MEAN, UNFRIENDLY FACES. I WAS ALWAYS TRYING TO SCARE PEOPLE AWAY. MRS. POTTS HELPS YOU WITH THAT.

SHE HAD ME DO THIS EXERCISE WHERE I THINK ABOUT SCORING A WINNING TOURNEY GOAL. I DID THAT AS MUCH AS I COULD, WHEREVER I COULD, AND IT REALLY DID MAKE ME LOOK NICER. WAY MORE PEOPLE CAME UP TO TALK TO ME.

HEROIC LEADERSHIP

(NOT OFFERED EVERY SEMESTER, TAUGHT BY BEAST)

Okay, I actually found this class SUPER helpful, and not just because I'm going to be queen one day. It teaches you the basic leadership skills you need to do well in positions of power. Like how to really listen to people, and how to manage your time, and how to tell the difference between good advice and bad advice. If you want to run a club at Auradon Prep or maybe become captain of the gymnastics or tourney team—this class is for you.

YOUR POSSIBLE-MAYBE-FUTURE SCHEDULE

MON./WED./FRI.	TUES./THURS.
REMEDIAL GOODNESS 101	DRAGON ANATOMY
MATHEMATICS	CHEMISTRY
DRAGON ANATOMY	LIFE SKILLS WITHOUT MAGIC
LUNCH	HEROIC LEADERSHIP
HISTORY OF AURADON	LUNCH
LIFE SKILLS WITHOUT MAGIC	UNABRIDGED FAIRY TALES FROM THE NINETEEN REGIONS
CHEMISTRY	REMEDIAL GOODNESS 101
UNABRIDGED FAIRY TALES FROM THE NINETEEN REGIONS	MATHEMATICS

WARNING, WARNING, WARNING: THESE ARE ABOUT 150 PAGES EACH. I'D GO WITH BELLE'S BOOK CLUB INSTEAD. THE WHOLE SEMESTER YOU READ THREE QUICK PAGE-TURNERS. BEANSTALKS AND OGRES AND STUFF. EVEN I KIND OF DUG THEM.

Fashion Emergency?

When Mal, Jay, Carlos, and I first came to Auradon, the other students were not into our Isle style. We'd always made the most of what we had available to create our own looks/styles. From our vibrant hair colors to our ripped hems and studded jackets, we brought a wickedly cool edge that was foreign to them.

EVIE'S 4 HEARTS

Mal's Cotillion Look

by Evie's 4 Hearts

Fortunately, you won't have to deal with that. With Mal making diplomatic visits around Auradon and all, everyone has seen her Isle style. Now people are begging to dress like her. We're seeing more dyed hair and ripped jeans all around Auradon. Feel free to wear your Isle clothes

at Auradon Prep, but make sure you clean them up first. The grungy, mud-caked look will never be in.

Carlos's Cotillion Look

by Evie's 4 Hearts ♡

Check out my other favorite looks.

EVIE'S 4 HEARTS

EVIE'S 4HEARTS

Every piece is made with love and care.

For more formal occasions, or a special Auradon-by-way-of-the-Isle look, I'm currently taking orders for custom clothes and accessories. Everything would be made to your measurements. Just allow four to six weeks for delivery.

FROM DORM ROOM
TO YOUR OWN
PERSONAL LAIR

When Evie and I got to Auradon, I was less than thrilled with our dorm room. It's on the second floor of the west wing (aka the girls' dormitory), and it looked like a fairy's nest exploded in it. Pink floral canopies, bedspreads, pillows, throw blankets, everything. Even worse, it had these huge windows that let sunlight in.

Now I'm used to Auradon decor. It's as bright and cheerful as Fairy Godmother herself. I even like the clear blue skies and sun. (Okay, LIKE is a strong word . . . I can tolerate it.) Since Evie and I were the only VK girls at Auradon Prep, they made us roomies. I guess you could request another roommate, but it makes sense for us VKs to stick together, right? Here's everything you need to know about dorm life at Auradon Prep . . . . .

—The second floor of the West Wing has great views of the quad and garden, but it's also REALLY SUNNY UP THERE. Might be better to room on the bottom floor if your eyes are still adjusting to the light.

—ROOMS 10, 22, and 19 in the West Wing are a little bigger than the other rooms.

—ROOMS 19, 20, 44, and 43 are all CORNER ROOMS, so there are windows on two walls.

—THE EAST WING, AKA THE BOYS' DORM, HAS A SECRET PASSAGEWAY TO THE DINING HALL. IT'S BEHIND THE BOOKCASE ON THE SECOND FLOOR—JUST PULL OUT THE COPY OF LITTLE RED RIDING HOOD.

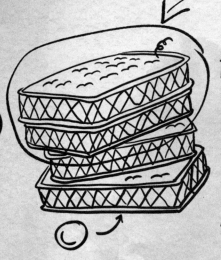

—FOR WHATEVER REASON, THE BEDS ON THE SECOND FLOOR OF THE BOYS' DORM ARE WAAAAAAAY COMFIER THAN THE ONES ON THE FIRST FLOOR. THERE'S A RUMOR OUR MATTRESSES ARE ONLY TWO YEARS OLD AND THEY GOT THEM FROM ABOVE THE PEA.

—CURFEW IS CRAZY STRICT. YOU CAN GET SUSPENDED OR EVEN EXPELLED IF YOU BREAK IT MORE THAN ONCE. BE IN YOUR ROOM, WITH THE LIGHTS OUT, BY 10 P.M.

—ROOMS 62 AND 87 IN THE EAST WING ARE BY FAR THE BIGGEST. ROOMS 65 AND 99 ARE CLOSEST TO THE COMMON AREA, SO THEY CAN BE NOISY. (I LIKE NOISE, BUT I GUESS A LOT OF AURADON KIDS DON'T?)

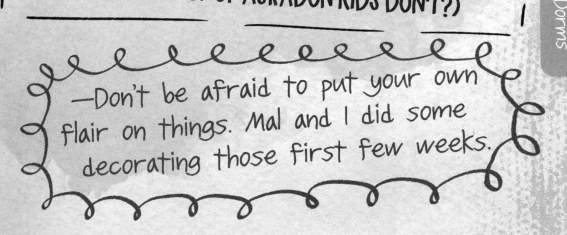

—Don't be afraid to put your own flair on things. Mal and I did some decorating those first few weeks.

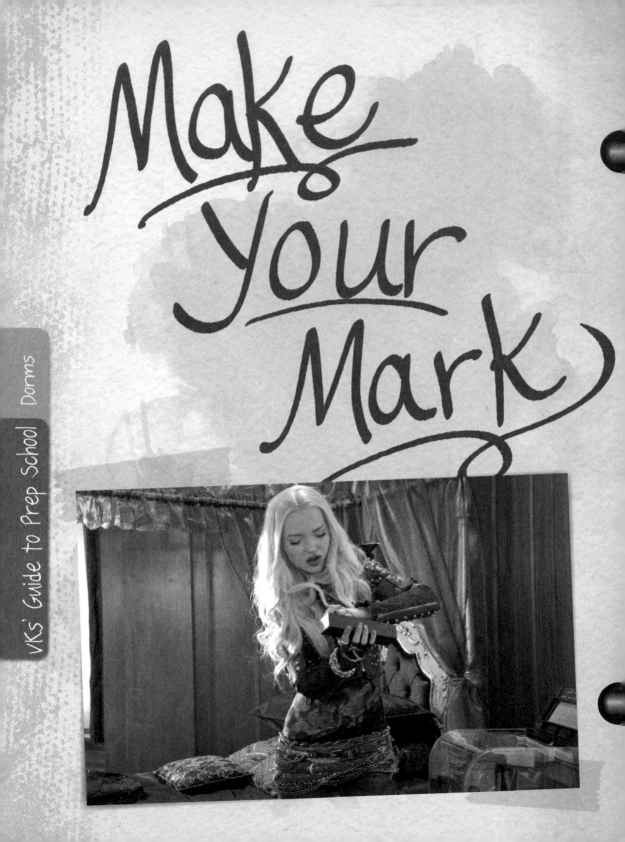

Make Your Mark

Like I said, it took a little while for Mal and me to get comfortable in our room. I loved it as soon as I walked in, but we spent weeks making it our own home. When you start decorating (or redecorating, really), keep these tips in mind. . . .

—Do check out Fairy Tale Fabrics. It's a block north of Belle's Harbor. They have rolls and rolls of every color and type of fabric you could imagine. I found it when I was shopping for Evie's 4 Hearts, and I tell everyone to use it for duvet covers and curtains.

—DON'T be afraid of bold colors. The Auradon Prep standard-issue sheets and comforters for the girls' dormitory are all pale pink and purple. We went with a bright blue for our new blankets and curtains.

—DO bring in your own Isle flair. We used to have these huge spray-painted murals at our hideout on the Isle, and I wanted to do something to re-create that. Obviously I couldn't spray-paint the walls, so I framed a painting in our Isle style and hung it on the wall.

—DO STRAIGHTEN UP. I'M NOT a NEAT FREAK OR ANYTHING, BUT ONE THING I LEARNED FROM LIVING IN AURADON IS THAT YOUR ROOM WILL ACTUALLY LOOK BETTER IF IT'S CLEAN(ISH). TRY TO AT LEAST KEEP YOUR CLOTHES OFF THE FLOOR.

—DON'T toss anything. If you're not going to use something in the room, store it in the closet or the extra storage units in the school basement.

—DON'T worry about your style being too "weird" or "different." Different is good. Being from the Isle is cool. Just do you.

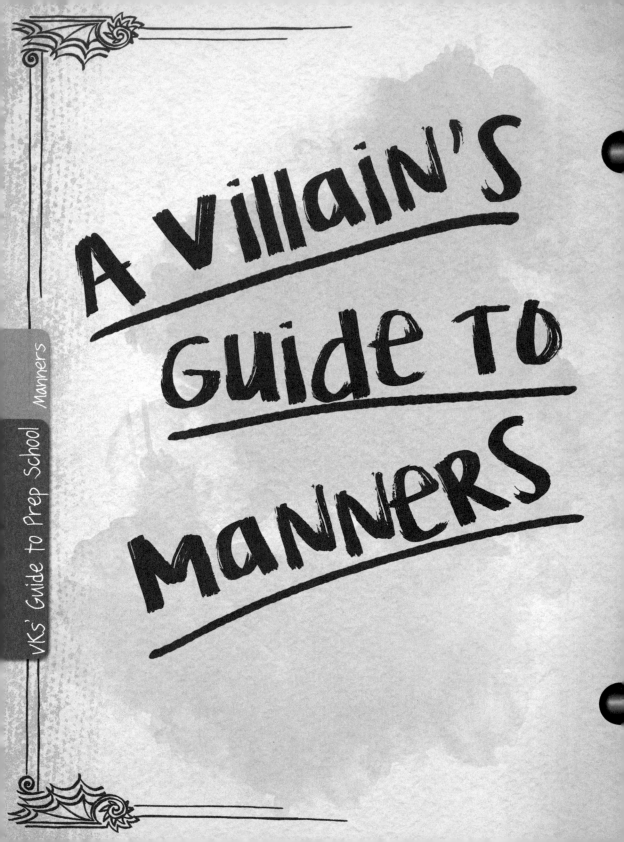

A Villain's Guide to Manners

If you're anything like me, you roll your eyes at the mention of manners and etiquette. Fairy Godmother made me read a whole stack of books about them after I got here. The truth is you do need to know **SOME** rules of etiquette if you're going to survive in Auradon. Kids here eat with forks and knives, and you can't just walk around with chocolate all over your mouth. (I'm looking at you, Carlos.)

HEY! I USE NAPKINS NOW! DON'T I GET AT LEAST SOME CREDIT FOR IMPROVEMENT?

USE THE FORK AND KNIFE TOGETHER TO CUT YOUR FOOD INTO SMALL BITES. IT'S NOT POLITE TO JUST SHOVE A HUGE CHUNK IN YOUR MOUTH.

The Lady's Guide to Setting the Table

Water glass

Goblet

Salad plate

Napkin

Salad fork

Dinner fork

Dinner plate

Dinner knife

Soupspoon

Dessert spoon

—WHEN YOU FIRST SIT DOWN TO EAT, PUT YOUR NAPKIN ON YOUR LAP. THE NAPKIN IS THE PIECE OF CLOTH THAT ALL THE UTENSILS SIT ON. USE IT WHENEVER YOU HAVE SOMETHING ON YOUR MOUTH. (JUST KIND OF WIPE THE STUFF OFF.)

—Saying please and thank you is customary in Auradon. These words are your new best friends.

—If someone walks past you and says hello or "How are you?" just smile and respond normally. The first time this happened to me, I grabbed my purse. I thought they were trying to distract me to steal my wallet.

—Try to hold the door open if someone's walking in behind you. I almost broke Lonnie's nose by not doing this.

THERE'S ONE THING I HAVE NEVER COMPLAINED ABOUT IN AURADON: THE FOOD. MRS. POTTS CAN COOK. PRETTY MUCH ANY MEAL YOU GET IN THE DINING HALL IS AMAZING. NO MOLD. NO MAGGOTS. NO STALE CRUSTS.

ON TUESDAYS YOU HAVE TO GET THE SPECIAL—CHIP'S GRILLED CHEESE. MRS. POTTS MAKES IT THE WAY HER SON LIKED IT GROWING UP. TWO PIECES OF CHEESE WITH A SLICE OF TOMATO IN THE CENTER. THIS MAY SOUND CRAZY, BUT I NEVER EVEN KNEW BREAD DIDN'T HAVE TO BE BURNT. HER GRILLED CHEESE IS ALWAYS THIS PERFECT GOLDEN BROWN, AND IT JUST MELTS IN YOUR MOUTH.

DON'T FORGET THE LAST FRIDAY OF THE MONTH! THAT'S WHEN THEY SET UP THE ICE CREAM SUNDAE BAR AT THE FAR END OF THE DINING HALL. UNLIMITED ICE CREAM SUNDAES. I'VE ALREADY FOUND MY WINNING COMBINATION: CHOCOLATE ICE CREAM, HOT FUDGE, CHOCOLATE SPRINKLES, AND CARAMEL SAUCE. THE SECRET IS YOU PUT THE CARAMEL SAUCE IN THE BOTTOM OF THE TALL ICE CREAM DISH, THEN MAKE THE SUNDAE ON TOP OF IT. IT'S BETTER THAN CANDY.

The winning combination is so obviously mint chocolate chip ice cream with hot fudge, whipped cream, and a cherry on top.

WE'RE GOING TO HAVE TO HAVE A TASTE TEST.

ERRRRR ... I HATE TESTS.

Sunday brunch is my favorite. Mrs. Potts puts out this incredible spread right at noon. Banana waffles, cinnamon buns, scones, and blueberry muffins. Sometimes she'll even make eggs Florentine, this fancy dish with sautéed spinach and poached eggs. She makes it with hollandaise sauce. It's so rich and creamy, it's like eating a stick of butter.

DON'T FORGET MONDAYS. THEY have BELLA NOTTE PASTA NIGHT. THEY dim THE LIGHTS and PUT FANCY WHITE TABLECLOTHS ON THE DINING TABLES. MRS. POTTS SERVES UP  EVERY KIND OF PASTA dish YOU CAN IMAGINE. CHEESE TORTELLINI, SPINACH RAVIOLI, MANICOTTI, AND, OF COURSE, SPAGHETTI AND MEATBALLS. MAYBE IT'S CHEESY (PUN INTENDED), BUT BEN AND I LOVE GOING TOGETHER AND SITTING AT ONE OF THE COZY TABLES IN THE CORNER.

LIKE JAY SAID—PRETTY MUCH EVERYTHING IS AMAZING.

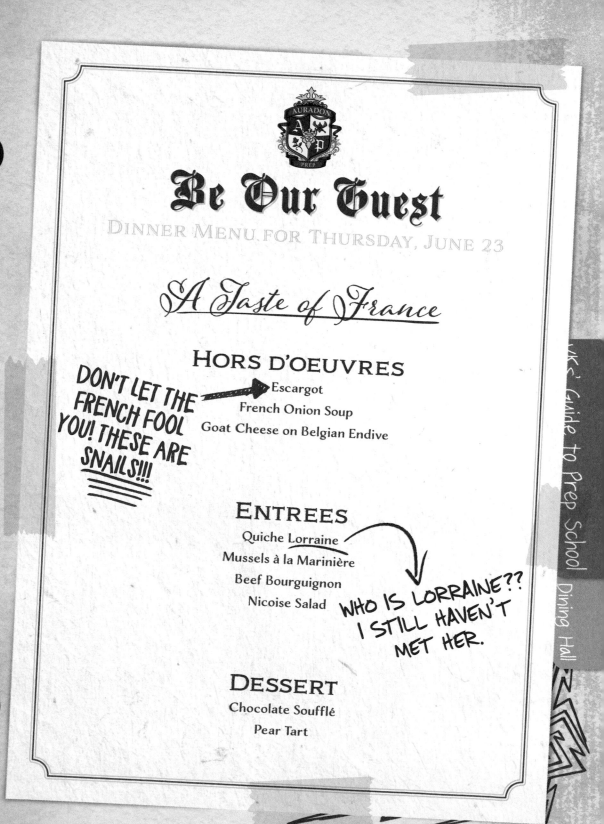

Be Our Guest

DINNER MENU FOR THURSDAY, JUNE 23

A Taste of France

HORS D'OEUVRES

Escargot

French Onion Soup

Goat Cheese on Belgian Endive

DON'T LET THE FRENCH FOOL YOU! THESE ARE SNAILS!!!

ENTREES

Quiche Lorraine

Mussels à la Marinière

Beef Bourguignon

Nicoise Salad

WHO IS LORRAINE?? I STILL HAVEN'T MET HER.

DESSERT

Chocolate Soufflé

Pear Tart

EVEN WHEN YOU'RE EATING THE BEST FOOD YOU'VE HAD IN YOUR LIFE, AND PEOPLE ARE SMILING ALL THE TIME AND BEING NICE TO YOU, IT CAN STILL BE HARD TO BE AWAY FROM THE ISLE. THOSE FIRST MONTHS I WAS HERE I THOUGHT ABOUT IT ALL THE TIME. I MISSED MY TREE HOUSE. I MISSED HELL HALL. I EVEN MISSED HOW COLD IT WAS THERE AND THE SOUND OF MY MOM YELLING AT ME FROM DOWNSTAIRS. CHANGE IS HARD, EVEN WHEN IT'S NECESSARY.

WE ALL HAVE DIFFERENT WAYS OF FIGHTING HOMESICKNESS. HERE ARE MINE:

HOW TO DEAL WITH HOMESICKNESS

—KEEP A PICTURE OF THE ISLE ON YOUR NIGHTSTAND OR DRESSER. THIS WAS MINE.

IT'LL REMIND YOU OF HOME.

—TALK TO OTHER VKS ABOUT THE GOOD TIMES YOU HAD ON THE ISLE. NOT EVERY DAY WAS A BAD DAY THERE.

—IF YOU'RE FEELING REALLY HOMESICK, GO DOWN TO THE DOCKS AT BELLE'S HARBOR. IT'S THE SAME SEA THAT'S ALL AROUND THE ISLE. THE AIR SMELLS LIKE HOME.

—I KEPT A DIARY THOSE FIRST MONTHS IN AURADON. IT REALLY HELPED ME THINK OF WHERE I WAS FROM AND WHERE I WAS GOING. MOVING AND STARTING A NEW SCHOOL CAN BE A LOT TO TAKE IN ALL AT ONCE.

MAL'S DIARY

—I WAS IN CONSTANT CONTACT WITH MY MOM THOSE FIRST WEEKS, MAINLY BECAUSE SHE WANTED ME TO DO HER EVIL BIDDING. I WOULDN'T RECOMMEND KEEPING IN TOUCH WITH YOUR PARENTS AT FIRST. GIVE YOURSELF A LITTLE TIME TO ADJUST.

—I keep something from the Isle with me at all times. Dizzy kept my original sketchbook for me when I first left the Isle and came to Auradon. Now that she's here and I have it again, I'm going to carry it with me. It has my very first designs. I made my first dress with old curtains my mom was getting rid of.

—Stay busy. Having my business helped distract me from thinking too much (or missing the Isle too much).

EVIE'S 4 HEARTS

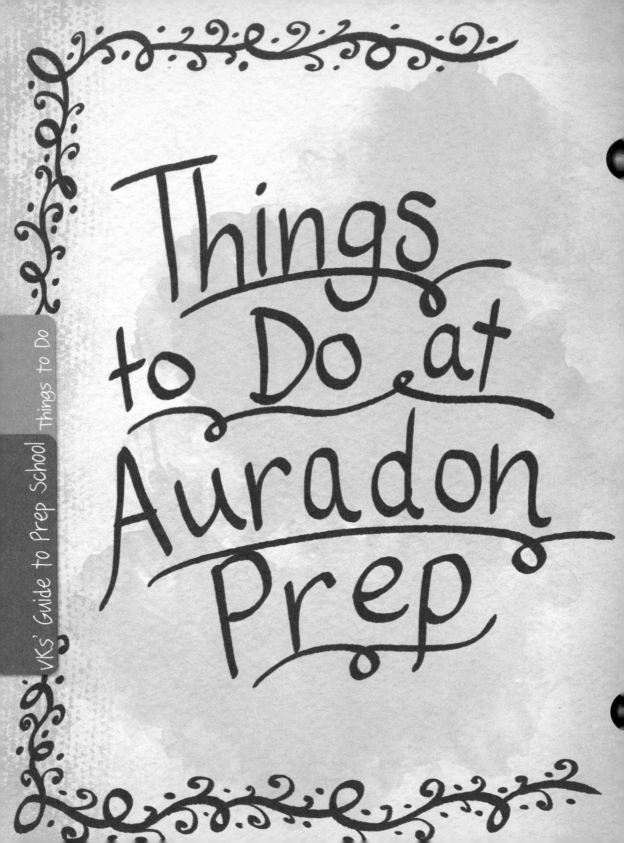

Things to Do at Auradon Prep

Okay, maybe you just got here and you don't have a design business to distract you but there are tons of ways to get involved at Auradon Prep. Campus life is its own fun thing. Since everyone lives at school, kids are always looking for things to do after class or on weekends. It's kind of impossible to be bored.

Dance till you Drop

This wicked dance party happens once a month. Kids from all over Auradon show up to compete in unofficial dance-offs in the Auradon Prep gymnasium. They have a DJ spinning until midnight, and dancers break out every kind of style you could imagine. It's pretty cool. Every time I go, I pick up new moves and sharpen my dance skills. I also (obviously) destroy the competition.

SHE DOES NOT lie (AT LEAST NOT ANYMORE).

TOURNEY, DUH

IF YOU HAVEN'T AT LEAST HEARD OF TOURNEY BY NOW, YOU'VE BEEN LIVING IN A CAVE (I GUESS THIS IS A REAL POSSIBILITY IF YOU'RE COMING FROM THE ISLE). THEY BROADCAST AURADON PREP TOURNEY GAMES ON THE AURADON NEWS NETWORK ALL THE TIME. YOU'VE PROBABLY ALREADY SEEN OUR TEAM FACING OFF AGAINST THE LOST BOYS OR THE SEASIDE MERMEN. THERE'S SPRINTING AND PASSING AND GIANT RED CANNONS THAT SHOOT DRAGON FIRE. IT'S PRETTY MUCH THE BEST SPORT IN THE NINETEEN REGIONS.

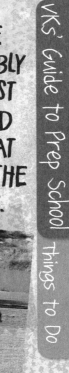

Fashion Forward Night

This happens every year in May. Auradon Prep students are big on "charitable giving," so they host an annual fashion show. Girls and guys wear different clothes from Auradon boutiques and then people bid on them. I may not be the only designer in Auradon, but I am the only one who gives away clothes at the fashion show. It's great advertising for me.

"CHARITABLE GIVING" WAS REALLY HARD FOR ME TO UNDERSTAND AT FIRST. THEY RAISE MONEY—MORE COIN THAN YOU COULD EVEN IMAGINE—AND THEN THEY JUST GIVE IT AWAY SO "FUND-RAISER" IS LIKE A FANCY WORD FOR GIVING AWAY COIN.

GADGETS AND GIZMOS

WE NEVER HAD COOL COMPUTERS, 3-D PRINTERS, VIDEO GAMES, OR SMARTPHONES ON THE ISLE. WHEN I GOT TO AURADON PREP, JAY AND I STARTED PLAYING VIDEO GAMES AND WE GOT A 3-D PRINTER. THAT'S WHEN I DISCOVERED HOW MUCH I LOVE TECH. DOUG TOLD ME ABOUT THIS CLUB. IT'S FOR TECHIE STUDENTS LIKE ME. WE TAKE APART ALL THE LATEST GADGETS AND GIZMOS AND THEN TEACH OURSELVES HOW TO PUT THEM BACK TOGETHER AGAIN. IT'S THIS COOL CRASH COURSE IN BUILDING AND REBUILDING THINGS. I'VE ALREADY LEARNED SO MUCH.

SWORDS AND SHIELDS

THE SWORDS AND SHIELDS TEAM HAS GONE FROM FIFTH IN THE USA TO NUMBER ONE IN JUST A FEW SHORT MONTHS, AND IT'S ALL BECAUSE OF LONNIE. SHE'S THE CAPTAIN OF THE TEAM NOW. HER SWORD SKILLS ARE THE BEST I'VE EVER SEEN (AND I'VE SEEN A LOT OF SWORD FIGHTS) AND SHE'S JUST AN INCREDIBLE LEADER, TOO. THERE'S ALWAYS BEEN THIS RULE ABOUT THE TEAM BEING "THE CAPTAIN AND EIGHT MEN," BUT I KNOW LONNIE WOULD TRY TO CHANGE THIS RULE IF ANY GIRL (FROM THE ISLE OR NOT) WANTED TO JOIN.

CANINE APPRECIATION DAY

SINCE DUDE'S BEEN ABLE TO TALK, HE'S BEEN BLABBERING NONSTOP ABOUT THIS. ALL DAY AND NIGHT, HE JUST KEPT HARASSING ME. "DOGS DON'T GET ANY RESPECT IN AURADON! HOW COME NOBODY TALKS ABOUT HOW OUR FORMER KING WAS BASICALLY A GIANT DOG? WHY DOESN'T ANYONE KNOW DOGS DON'T LIKE BELLY RUBS RIGHT AFTER THEY EAT?"

I FINALLY CAVED AND ASKED FAIRY GODMOTHER IF WE COULD HAVE CANINE APPRECIATION DAY EVERY SEPTEMBER 12. NOW STUDENTS SHARE PICTURES OF THEIR DOGS AND TELL STORIES ABOUT THEIR DOGS, AND BELLE USUALLY DOES A WHOLE BIG POST ON BEAST. #AURADONLOVESCANINES

EVENT and PARTY PLANNING COMMITTEE WITH JANE

If you want to dive into life at Auradon Prep, join the Event and Party Planning Committee. Jane runs it, and they plan all these events throughout the year. They're the ones who put together Cotillion and Family Day, and some of the parties that happened after the Coronation. Jane has already started asking me what kinds of flowers I want for the party after I'm crowned queen (she's more organized than Evie's closet).

cheer squad

If you want to cheer on the tourney and swords and shields teams, you can join Jane on this squad. It's totally not my thing, but some people like it.

Auradon pro tip: If you keep your schedule really busy, there won't be any time for thieving or plotting evil deeds. That's definitely a good thing.

The New Recruits

This next part is all YOU. Share your stories. Why'd you want to go to Auradon Prep? What was your application process like? Do you have questions for us VK upperclassmen and graduates?

OF COURSE THEY DO.

Dizzy Tremaine

Forever Dreamin'

Oh, you probably won't believe this but I actually remember every single tiny detail about the day I heard I'd been admitted to Auradon Prep. I'd been watching the Cotillion on the Auradon News Network on the old TV in my granny's salon. Obviously I was freaking out when Evie mentioned me and my headpieces. I think I actually shrieked and jumped up and down. It was all this crazy rush of excitement and me thinking how cool it was that girls in Auradon were wearing my designs and everything, and then my granny yelled for me to keep it down because she was taking a nap.

I kept watching, though, and I saw the whole battle between Uma and Mal, which was also pretty nuts because I've, like, grown up on the Isle with both of them. Later, I was doing my chores. I usually put my headphones on when I do them and just listen to music. So I was listening to music and sweeping and then I turned around and there were these two royal guards in yellow-and-blue uniforms standing in the doorway. At first I thought it was a joke or something (everyone is always playing pranks on the Isle), but then they handed me the official announcement. I thought my heart was going to explode.

This is it! This is the actual invitation the royal guards gave me that day, on this fancy scroll and everything. I mean, there was actually more to the story that I didn't really realize at the time, but I was still freaking out

His Royal Majesty King Ben of Auradon and Ms. Evie of the Isle request the pleasure of your company, Dizzy Tremaine, for the upcoming academic year at Auradon Prep. Please notify His Majesty's royal couriers of your response to this request.

We'd love you to join us at Auradon Prep. Will you come?

King Ben

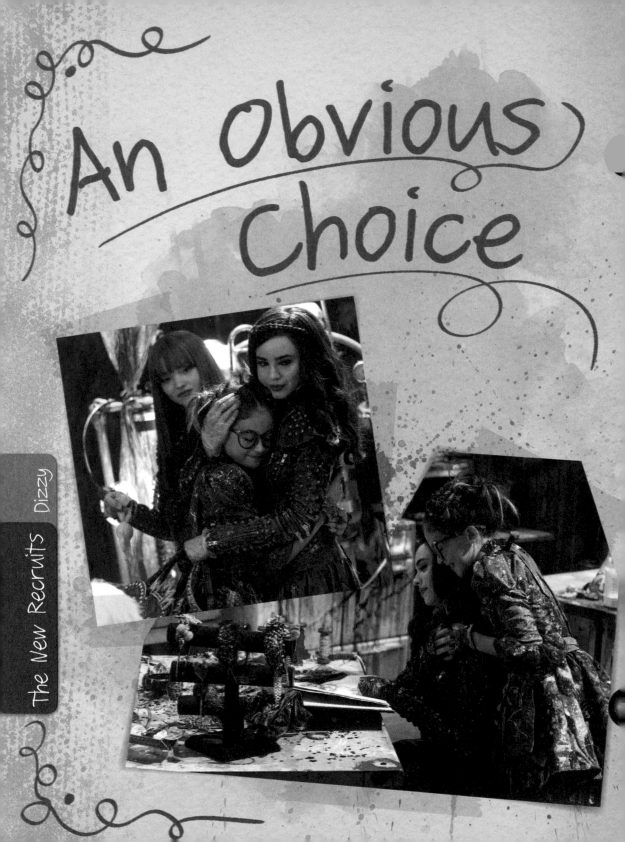

An obvious Choice

It's true: even after Dizzy got this invitation from King Ben, she had to put in an official application to be fair to the other villain kids. Ben wanted everyone who came over from the Isle of the Lost to write an essay about what coming to Auradon would mean to them. He wanted them to give details of their history and their goals for the upcoming school year. We tried to avoid kids who wanted to continue their wicked ways.

But Dizzy always stood out in my mind as one of the most deserving kids from the Isle. She worked hard at her grandmother's shop, Lady Tremaine's Curl Up and Dye, and she never complained. She's somehow managed to stay optimistic even after fourteen years on the Isle. That and she's crazy talented. She just has this incredible eye for color and design. I mean, did you see those Cotillion headpieces?!

APPLICATION *for* AURADON PREP

Children of the Isle of the Lost! Mal and King Ben invite you to meet them and the other villain kids formerly of the Isle at Auradon Prep to enroll you for the upcoming scholastic year. By filling out this application form you will be eligible to become part of the second wave of villain kids that will help to reunite our divided kingdom.

Please complete this form as accurately as you can. Our goal is to welcome all of the children of the Isle of the Lost to Auradon as expeditiously as possible. At this time, however, we will only be accepting four more. Mal and King Ben ask you to be truthful, sincere and to always speak from your heart. In time, we will all be together as one nation. Your courage in volunteering for this program will bring that day closer! Best of luck!

Dizzy Tremaine
_____
Name

None
_____
Known aliases

Diz or Dee
_____
Nicknames or other

November 28. (I'm fourteen.)
_____
Date of birth or best guess

Isle of the Lost
Place of birth

Anything neon (pink, green, yellow, blue)
Favorite color

Designing clothes and headpieces, listening to music
Favorite activity

Artists and thieves (I only like the artist part, though)
Favorite school subject

Drizella Tremaine.   But in case of emergencies, contact my granny, Lady Tremaine.
Parents' names (or aliases)

My mom is a socialite, and runs the Wicked Beauties club at Serpent Prep.
My granny owns Curl Up and Dye salon.
Parents' profession(s)

Who is your favorite of the first wave of VKs? There is no wrong answer.

I have to choose Evie! She's one of my best friends.

AURADON

In your own words, tell us why you want to come to Auradon. There is no wrong answer.

So most of my days are spent at school or in my granny's salon, sweeping up hair and wiping down the mirrors and sinks. I didn't really know that coming to Auradon would ever be an option for me, but then Evie left, and I'd watch her on TV all the time and follow her adventures there, and all of a sudden it all seemed possible. Like, maybe I could go to Auradon one day too. Maybe I could start fresh and have all these great opportunities. For the first time I really started dreaming about what my life could be and what I could do if I only got the chance.

I started spending the tiny bit of free time I had drawing in my sketchbook. I designed all these cool headpieces, and then I'd scour the alleys and dumpsters on the Isle, looking for different materials I could make them out of. Old fabric, wire, mattress springs, gemstones, beads, fishing nets, nuts and bolts—anything that seemed hip and unusual.

I painted them and would wear them around the salon to make sure they were comfortable and could, like, really be a thing. Anyway, I'm sure Evie told you all this already because you sent me that invitation, but I think I deserve the opportunity to come to Auradon because I'm really focused on doing better. On not just doing good, but doing the very best I can.

I look forward to hearing from you!   Oh! I almost forgot! I've included sketches of a few of my custom headpiece designs.

Congratulations on completing the application. Mal, Jay, Evie, and Carlos will collect it on the appointed date and announce the next of many villain kids who will join them in Auradon. If you are not picked, please don't despair. In time all of you will join us and help make our world whole again!

Dizzy Tremaine

Signature

Please place
thumbprint here

Wow. It's so weird to reread my application after all this time. . . .

So I'm finally here in Auradon (YAY!) and I get to spend the summer living off campus in Evie's castle. When the school year starts, I'll move into the dorms. When Evie asked me if I wanted to come live with her, I didn't even hesitate. It just seemed like a perfect idea. Not only do I get to hang out with Evie every day, but I get to be in her really cool creative sanctuary. It's going to be so easy here to make art and just have fun inventing.

So much is possible in Auradon. Don't be afraid to set big goals for yourself. Ambition (that just means wanting to achieve a lot) is your friend.

So Excited!

I've never really ventured very far from my granny's salon, so getting invited to Auradon was a really big deal. I couldn't believe it was actually happening, that I was actually leaving the Isle of the Lost. When I got into the limo and went through the barrier for the first time, my heart was beating so fast and I could barely breathe.

I mean, I've seen Auradon from the shores of the Isle of the Lost, but when we stepped out, I was pretty amazed how beautiful it is! I could smell the fresh air and feel the warm sun on my skin. And maybe this sounds silly, but I love the idea of just sitting in the grass here! I never even knew grass was a thing before, but it's so great to feel how soft and cushiony and cool it is underneath you, like this mattress of squishy goodness. Picnicking is going to be my new favorite hobby.

DON'T FORGET: SUNSCREEN.

Roger that.

I REMEMBER GETTING OUT OF THE LIMO FOR THE FIRST TIME. I'D BEEN EATING THIS CHOCOLATE BAR IN THE BACK SEAT AND THEN I STEPPED OUT AND ALL OF A SUDDEN IT WAS: SUNLIGHT! BEN! HEROES AND THEIR KIDS!! AURADON PREP! BEAST STATUE!

IT WAS CRAZY OVERWHELMING.

Time to Shine

When I left for Auradon, my granny said she just wanted what was best for me. Since I won't be working at her salon all the time, I'll have these huge chunks of time to figure out what that is. I can just sit by the Enchanted Lake or take a nap or sketch all my new headpiece designs. I mean, I'm going to have so much free time and energy, I can even help Evie do some of the initial cutting and sewing on her Evie's 4 Hearts line. She can really show me the ropes.

I KNOW WHAT YOU MEAN. I SPENT SO MUCH TIME WORKING AT MY DAD'S JUNK SHOP THAT I NEVER HAD ANY ME TIME. NOW I'M ON THE TOURNEY TEAM AND SWORDS AND SHIELDS AND I EVEN STUDY (DON'T TELL ANYONE, THOUGH).

THINGS TO DO WITH ME TIME

- NAP

- FIND A HOBBY OR A SPORT

- EAT LUNCH OR DINNER WITH YOUR FRIENDS

- TAKE A WALK OUTSIDE

- WATCH TV

- JUST BE A TEENAGER AND HAVE FUN !!!

Celia Facilier

Goodness Ain't Easy

Just Another Day

You know that giddy, happy feeling everyone always talks about when they mention Auradon? I don't get it. I mean, sure, it sounds nice, but the Isle is my home. I heard Mal was coming back to the Isle of the Lost to choose some new recruits for Auradon Prep. You had to fill out an application and write an essay and all that jazz. But I never was all teary-eyed about it. I just assumed I wouldn't be chosen. I almost didn't apply. Then I figured all those Auradon kids would want to know their happily ever after. I could read their fortunes with my fortune cards! There's a lot of coin to be made reading fortunes in Auradon City.

But I still wasn't totally convinced. Then Dizzy told me she was applying, and I was behind Clay Clayton in the market and he was talking about it, too. For a straight week, it seemed like everyone was blabbering on about Auradon Prep, and VK Day, and how Mal and Evie and Jay and Carlos were coming to save us all. I didn't like the thought that my friends would be leaving without me. So I just filled out an application. I figured, what the hey?

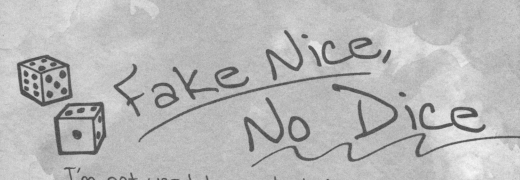

Fake Nice, No Dice

I'm not used to people being nice. It's not normal to always be smiling and asking how your day is going. I can't help thinking it's fake. Like, what's your hustle? I've only just arrived in Auradon, and I keep thinking not everyone can be this nice. I just don't buy it.

I DIDN'T TRUST ANYONE EITHER WHEN I CAME HERE. IT ALL SEEMED SO PHONY. IT'S NOT. IT JUST TAKES TIME TO GET USED TO....

The Isle

THE BAD

VK DAY!
FOUR MORE TO GO

Rumor has it another four villain kids will be dragged off the Isle of the Lost today as a determined King Ben continues his horrible plan to bring more Isle kids to Auradon Prep. Though many Isle of the Lost children have filled out essays and applications, hoping to go to Auradon, concerned citizens have expressed distrust of and outrage over the program, which was just implemented last year.

"They took my son, and no one says a word about it," Jafar, owner of the market junk shop, said in a statement to the

Tribune

NEWS

Tribune. "Now I have to pay someone to steal for me. It cuts into my profits."

"I heard there's sunshine and birds in Auradon," a woman who asked to remain anonymous said. "What, am I supposed to be impressed? Who wants that? Yuck."

+ Apparently a lot of naive children who don't know any better do. Dozens have submitted their applications. Lady Mal, daughter of Maleficent, returns to the Isle of the Lost today with Evie, daughter of the Evil Queen; Jay, son of Jafar; and Carlos, son of Cruella De Vil, to announce the students who will be admitted for the new school year. To those traitorous souls: bad luck!

APPLICATION for AURADON PREP

Children of the Isle of the Lost! Mal and King Ben invite you to meet them and the other villain kids formerly of the Isle at Auradon Prep to enroll you for the upcoming scholastic year. By filling out this application form you will be eligible to become part of the second wave of villain kids that will help to reunite our divided kingdom.

Please complete this form as accurately as you can. Our goal is to welcome all of the children of the Isle of the Lost to Auradon as expeditiously as possible. At this time, however, we will only be accepting four more. Mal and King Ben ask you to be truthful, sincere and to always speak from your heart. In time, we will all be together as one nation. Your courage in volunteering for this program will bring that day closer! Best of luck!

Celia Facilier

Name
_____

Skullz

Known aliases
_____

CeeCee

Nicknames or other
_____

October 31 (I'm thirteen.)

Date of birth or best guess
_____

Isle of the Lost
Place of birth

Purple, pink, orange, green—
anything bright and colorful
Favorite color

Fortune-telling
Favorite activity

Scheme Management 101
Favorite school subject

Dr. Facilier
Parents' names (or aliases)

Headmaster of Dragon Hall, arcade owner, scheming bocor
Parents' profession(s)

Who is your favorite of the first wave of VKs? There is no wrong answer.

I've always admired Jay's thievery.

In your own words, tell us why you want to come to Auradon. There is no wrong answer.

Auradon sounds cool and all. I heard everyone else was applying so I decided to apply, too. Someone told me, "You've got to be in it to win it." So this is me being in it to win it. Now can I please take an Auradon Prep vacation????

P.S.: I made these fortune-telling cards myself. I used some old watercolors I found down by the wharf and just kind of painted them or whatever. They're fine, I guess. I just thought maybe I should show you.

Fortune-Telling for Beginners

You can't say a villain kid doesn't know what success is. Because there's one thing I did well—really well—on the Isle of the Lost. I can read fortune cards. I can tell someone a fortune so spot-on their eyes pop out of their heads, and they give me this look like, How'd you know that?!?

The cards never lie.

You can make a (kind of) honest living from reading fortune cards. Here are a few of my favorite cards and what they mean if you pull them from my deck. . . .

The Empress
Look for opportunities to be generous and kind.

The Fool
Trust your instincts.

Ace of Swords
You are clear about what you need to accomplish.

Journey
A new adventure/fresh start is coming your way!

JOURNEY

There's one thing that Auradon Prep definitely doesn't have: my dad as its headmaster. When you're the headmaster's kid, the school is your rotten oyster. You can start food fights, lift jewelry from lockers, skip classes, and hang out with your friends in the dungeons. And if you get caught, what are they going to do? Send you to your parent's office!

OKAY. THIS DOES SOUND PRETTY AWESOME. I'M NOT GOING TO PRETEND IT DOESN'T. WE ALL KNOW YOU HAD IT GOOD AT DRAGON HALL. BUT I THINK EVENTUALLY YOU'LL SEE AURADON PREP HAS WAAAAAAAY MORE TO OFFER YOU.

What I'll Miss About Being the Headmaster's Kid

—Sneaking into the Athenaeum of Evil whenever I wanted (I think I'm the only person who knows where Dad hides the key.)

—Never carrying a hall pass

—Taking naps on the couch in my dad's office (I used to go there between classes or after school.)

—Never having to go to Evil Schemes and Nasty Plots (Lady Tremaine teaches this class and I can't stand the sound of her voice. What. A. Drama. Queen.)

—Not caring about my report card

—Class starting at noon (This has nothing to do with being the headmaster's kid—it's just something I'm going to really miss.)

I MEAN, I'M GOING TO COLLEGE NEXT FALL. HOW NUTS IS THAT?!?

I KNOW YOU loved DRAGON Hall, but WORK WiTH US, Celia. YOU CAN CHOOSE good if YOU Really TRY. AND if YOU'RE having TROUBLE figuring OUT what a "good" CHOICE iS and what WOULD BE CONSIDERED a "bad" choice, HERE'S aN Easy guide.

DOES iT SOUND like iT WON'T BE VERY FUN?

YES   NO

WOULD iT HURT SOMEONE'S FEELINGS?

YES   NO

WOULD YOUR dad BE PROUD OF YOU FOR doing iT?

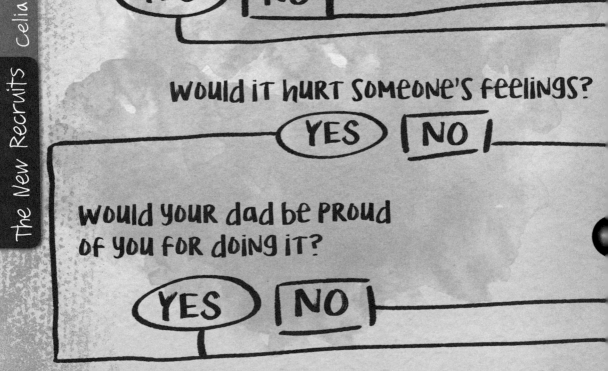

YES   NO

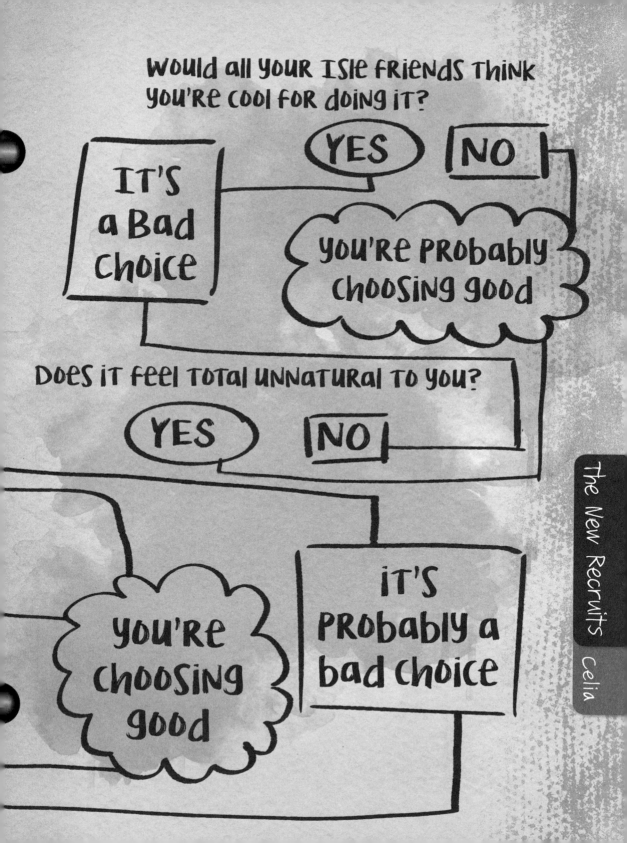

Squeaky

and Squirmy

The Little Guys

Our dad really wanted us to apply for Auradon Prep. It's not like things were that great for me and Squirmy on the Isle. Everyone thinks of us as Smee's kids, two tiny nerds who don't really matter at all.

Now that I'm here, I'm going to sign up for the debate club, the chess club, and marching band. I went over my schedule with Doug and he checked and double-checked that I was taking all the best classes with all the best teachers. Maybe I won't be as popular as Mal or a star athlete like Jay, but I know there's a place for me here. I can feel it.

THERE DEFINITELY IS. YOU SHOULD CHECK OUT THE ASTRONOMY CLUB, TOO. ONCE A MONTH THEY GO TO RAPUNZEL'S TOWER TO STARGAZE. AZIZ, ALADDIN AND JASMINE'S SON, IS IN IT, AND HE SAID IT'S REALLY COOL.

I wasn't really sure if applying was a good idea, but Squeaky's my older brother (by four minutes) and he said it was. I'm glad I believed him. There are no bullies here!

What We WILL Miss About the Isle

- Fishing trips with Dad

- The smell of the ocean

- How cool and damp it was under the deck, even in the summer

- Not having to wear sunscreen/sunglasses

- Ohhhh definitely the chocolate crepes at Frollo's Creperie

- We'll miss Dad, because he really wasn't the worst father a villain could have. Maybe not the best, but not the worst, either, right, Squeaky? Right.

What We WON'T Miss About the Isle

—Harry Hook stealing my squid snacks

—Getting seasick on choppy nights on the boat

—Not being able to concentrate at school because everyone is goofing around and making trouble

—Having to always stay together because two is better than one (safety in numbers!)

—Not being taken seriously

—Gil's hard-boiled-egg breath

APPLICATION *for* AURADON PREP

Children of the Isle of the Lost! Mal and King Ben invite you to meet them and the other villain kids formerly of the Isle at Auradon Prep to enroll you for the upcoming scholastic year. By filling out this application form you will be eligible to become part of the second wave of villain kids that will help to reunite our divided kingdom.

Please complete this form as accurately as you can. Our goal is to welcome all of the children of the Isle of the Lost to Auradon as expeditiously as possible. At this time, however, we will only be accepting four more. Mal and King Ben ask you to be truthful, sincere and to always speak from your heart. In time, we will all be together as one nation. Your courage in volunteering for this program will bring that day closer! Best of luck!

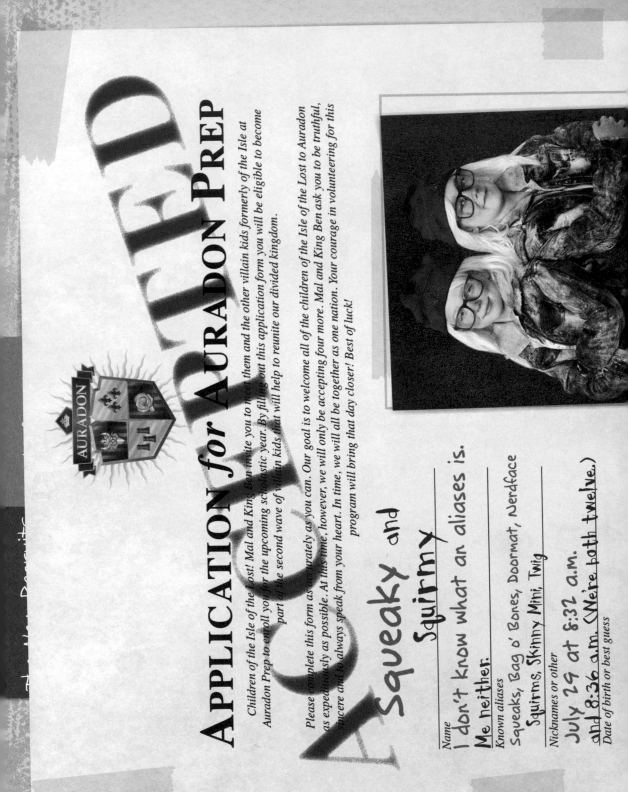

Name

I don't know what an aliases is. Me neither.

Known aliases

Squeaks, Bag o' Bones, Doormat, Nerdface Squirms, Skinny Mini, Twig

Nicknames or other

July 29 at 8:32 a.m. and 8:36 a.m. (We're both twelve.)

Date of birth or best guess

Dad's pirate ship on the Isle of the Lost
Place of birth

Blue stripes   Green
Favorite color

Reading   I just nap while Squeaky reads. I like hanging out belowdecks, away from all the noise (and bullies) on the wharf.
Favorite activity

Everything: history of the wharf; tall tales and the tellers who tell them; underwater science
Underwater science and math
Favorite school subject

Smee
Parents' names (or aliases)

Bosun, pirate, sidekick
Parents' profession(s)

Who is your favorite of the first wave of VKs? There is no wrong answer.

Carlos. Definitely.
Yeah. He was always so nice to us.

In your own words, tell us why you want to come to Auradon. There is no wrong answer.

Growing up, I never even knew what it meant to be a "sidekick." Kids would always say, "your dad's a sidekick," like it was an insult. Sometimes they'd call him a "minion." But we would just shrug and walk away.

Now that I'm older, I've realized it means you're not the hero of your own story. My dad spent so much of his life working for Captain Hook, cleaning his ship, plotting with him, and helping him do his evil deeds. We want more than that. We want to be the heroes in our stories and not have to stand in anyone's shadow anymore. We want a chance to succeed.

Yeah, what he said. We want to be better than what the Isle will let us be.

_____

_____

_____

_____

_____

_____

Congratulations on completing the application. Mal, Jay, Evie, and Carlos will collect it on the appointed date and announce the next of many villain kids who will join them in Auradon. If you are not picked, please don't despair. In time all of you will join us and help make our world whole again!

Squeaky Squirmy
—————————
Signature

Please place thumbprint here

We obviously sorted through dozens of applications, but I knew we had to let Squeaky and Squirmy in when I read that part about being the hero of your own story. It's strange, but it's like Squeaky was able to put into words what I had always felt about my life on the Isle of the Lost. I was always the daughter of the Evil Queen, plotting for her, taking her advice no matter how bad it was. I'd kind of gone on autopilot, you know? Just following everything she told me to do . . .

Coming to Auradon was a chance to be my own person. The hero of my own story (though I'd never really thought of it that clearly). I wasn't just free from the barrier, I was free from everything that had been holding me back—my mom, the expectation of evil, the idea that I had villainy in my blood.

Also, Squeaky and Squirmy are genuinely sweet. Kids like that don't stand a chance on the Isle of the Lost. They'll always be bullied. No one will ever take them seriously as long as they think they're "soft" or "weak." I knew they had to leave the Isle before it ruined them forever.

YEAH, IT WOULD'VE TURNED THEM INTO SOMETHING THEY'RE NOT. THAT'S WHAT HAPPENED TO ME, EVENTUALLY.

IT'S NOT EASY TO BE ON AURADON ALONE, WITHOUT YOUR PARENTS OR ALL THE FAMILIAR PLACES YOU GREW UP WITH ON THE ISLE OF THE LOST. I KNOW THAT AS MUCH AS ANYONE. NO MATTER HOW GREAT MY LIFE IS NOW, I STILL THINK OF THE ISLE AND THE WORLD I LEFT BEHIND. BUT IF I HADN'T COME TO AURADON PREP, I NEVER WOULD'VE MET BEN. I NEVER WOULD'VE CHOSEN A DIFFERENT PATH AND FINALLY GOTTEN MY MOM'S VOICE OUT OF MY HEAD. I NEVER WOULD'VE MADE ALL THESE INCREDIBLE NEW MEMORIES, EITHER. LIKE TURNING INTO A DRAGON AND WINNING THAT BATTLE AGAINST UMA.

COME ON, YOU HAVE TO ADMIT THAT WAS COOL.

IT WAS.

FIRE CAME OUT OF YOUR NOSE.

BUT SERIOUSLY: ONE OF THE BEST PARTS OF COMING TO AURADON PREP IS REWRITING YOUR STORY . . . AND FINDING . . .

The Good Times

That day with Ben, at the Enchanted Lake, was one of the first moments when I thought, maybe, just maybe, I might like living on Auradon. It was hard not to notice how pretty everything is here. I mean, on the Isle I'd never even heard a chirping bird, and on Auradon there's whole choruses of them.

And I mean, Ben IS pretty cute.

I KNOW WHAT YOU MEAN. FOR ME ALL THESE LITTLE MOMENTS STARTED TO PILE UP. LIKE WHEN I MET DUDE AND HE DIDN'T ACTUALLY RIP MY THROAT OUT. OR THIS ONE NIGHT WHEN DUDE AND I HAD THIS HUGE FIVE-HOUR TALK ABOUT THE MEANING OF LIFE AND HOW IT FEELS TO BE TWO FEET TALL AND HAVE FUR AND ALL THAT STUFF. OR THAT TIME I ASKED JANE TO COTILLION AND SHE SAID YES.

My favorite memories are easy: Mal and me lying on our beds our first months here, laughing about how Fairy Godmother says "Oh my!" whenever she's mad or overwhelmed. Or getting this crazy beautiful bouquet of flowers from Doug for Cotillion. Or just any of those afternoons when somehow Carlos, Mal, Jay, and I would all find our way onto the quad and hang out until the sun went down.

And Doug. Did I mention my favorite memory is anything that includes Doug? ♥

EVERY GOAL I EVER SCORED IN TOURNEY. OR HOW COACH JENKINS CAME UP TO ME AT THE END OF THE LAST TOURNAMENT AND TOLD ME HE WAS PROUD OF ME. NO ONE'S EVER SAID THAT TO ME BEFORE. I HAD NO IDEA WHAT IT EVEN MEANT.

ALSO, PRETTY MUCH EVERY RIDE IN THE LIMO IS GREAT. I DON'T THINK ROLLING UP TO AURADON PREP IN THAT LIMO WILL EVER GET OLD. I STILL REMEMBER THE FIRST TIME WE WENT THROUGH THE BARRIER AND I SAW THE SCHOOL AHEAD OF ME THROUGH THE WINDSHIELD.

Good Times

So what's next? Now it's time for you to start making memories of your own. Get settled in your dorm rooms, start classes, and begin your new lives. It's time for you to write your own stories.

SURE, IT'S GONNA BE A LITTLE WEIRD AT FIRST. YOU JUST HAVE TO FIGURE OUT YOUR WAY AROUND. LIKE YOU, I SPENT THE FIRST SIXTEEN YEARS OF MY LIFE ON THE ISLE. I KNEW EVERY STREET BY HEART. IT JUST TAKES A LITTLE WHILE.

AND REMEMBER, YOU HAVE EACH OTHER. I DON'T KNOW WHAT I WOULD HAVE DONE WITHOUT MAL, EVIE, AND JAY.

YOU MIGHT have chosen bad before, but now you have the OPPORTUNITY FOR SOMETHING better. YOUR life iS going to CHange, Starting today. BUT NeVer FOrGet where you came FROM. REMEMBER, We Villain KiDS always have TO STiCK TOGETHER!

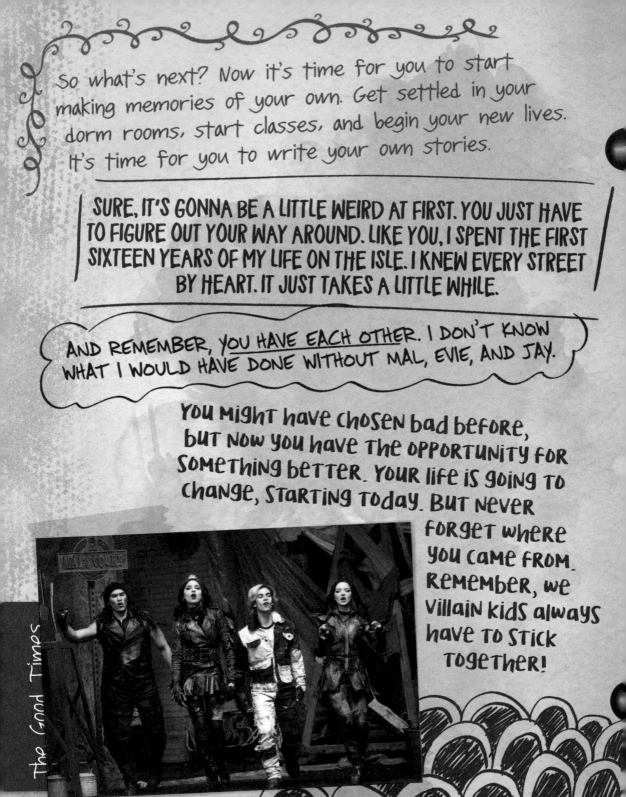

The Good Times